Juliet had to ob

She had no other ch... ...lips quickly covered hers and his hands drew her even closer to his hard body. She had not expected him to be touching her like this or kissing her again, and the shock of it momentarily stunned her with questions. But as his mouth began to move hungrily over hers, the whys quickly fled her mind. She couldn't wonder what was going on in his head. All she could do was experience the exquisite taste of his lips.

Jerking his head up, Matt quickly glanced over his shoulder.

"Some of the guests are leaving. We'd better get back."

His voice was thick and husky, telling Juliet he'd been just as lost in the moment as she.

Dear Reader,

Have you ever felt as though everything in your life has gone wrong? That even if you tried to make things better, you figure it would only make them worse? I'm fairly certain we've all fallen into that hopeless pit at one time or another and my hero, Matt Sanchez, is no exception.

When Neil Rankin first traveled from New Mexico down to south Texas and discovered a family of Ketchum cousins, I was intrigued with the whole bunch. In spite of their wealth, life hadn't necessarily been easy for any of them. But it was Matt Sanchez, the manager of the Sandbur Ranch, who particularly touched my heart. He was a tortured soul and needed help in the worst kind of way. I figured it was going to take a miracle to pull him up from that dark place where he'd been living.

What kind of miracle did Matt need? I asked myself. Maybe a lightning bolt from a clear blue sky to open his eyes? Or perhaps a near death escape would make him see the preciousness of life? Maybe he needed to lose everything he had in order to shock him back to the living? Fortunately, nothing that drastic was required. Love was all it took to put the light of hope back in Matt's heart. I hope you enjoy reading how he found it!

God bless, and may you never ride lonesome!

STELLA BAGWELL
THE RANCHER'S REQUEST

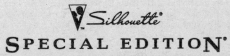

SPECIAL EDITION

Published by Silhouette Books

America's Publisher of Contemporary Romance

 SILHOUETTE BOOKS

ISBN-13: 978-0-373-28050-6
ISBN-10:   0-373-28050-5

THE RANCHER'S REQUEST

Copyright © 2007 by Stella Bagwell

This edition published by arrangement with Harlequin Books S.A.

® and TM are trademarks of Harlequin Books S.A., used under license.
Trademarks indicated with ® are registered in the United States Patent
and Trademark Office, the Canadian Trade Marks Office and in other
countries.

Visit Silhouette Books at www.eHarlequin.com

Printed in U.S.A.

STELLA BAGWELL

began writing romance novels over twenty years ago. Now, more than sixty books later, she likens her job to childbirth. The pain is great, but the rewards are too sweet to measure.

Over thirty-five years ago Stella married her high school sweetheart, and now the two live on the south Texas coast where the climate is tropical and the lifestyle blessedly slow. When Stella isn't at her desk, spinning out tales of love, she's usually working outdoors on their little ranch, 6 Pines, helping her husband care for a herd of very spoiled horses.

They have a son, who is a high school math teacher and athletic coach.

To my husband, Harrell, who has been
my own cowboy for nearly thirty-six years.
We'll ride the trail together and always.

Chapter One

Matt Sanchez hated weddings. In his opinion, the sentimental ceremonies were only a reminder of everything that could go wrong in a person's life and normally he made a point to steer clear of any social function with a white dress, tossed rice and weeping women. But the wedding of Raine Ketchum and Neil Rankin was one he couldn't avoid. The bride was his cousin and he loved her. Even if he would have preferred to saddle up his favorite horse and ride to the far end of the Sandbur Ranch, he couldn't miss the most important day of her life.

Thankfully, the exchange of vows had taken place more than an hour ago and now the Saddler house, the original ranch house on the Sandbur, was brimming with guests and relatives, some of whom had traveled all the way from New Mexico. Wedding cake was still being served and champagne, beer and punch were flowing like the San Antonio River after a spring flood.

In the great room, the rugs had been rolled back and the wooden floor sprinkled with cornmeal to make boots slide gracefully as couples danced to a four-piece band. Music, laughter and loud conversations collided, then ricocheted off the wood-beamed ceilings before they filled every nook and corner of the house.

At any other time, the reception would have been held outside, beneath the live oaks that graced the backyard. But February weather in South Texas could be fickle. Normally it was splendid with bright sunshine and temperatures just mild enough to make a person forget the long, blistering heat of the past seven months. Even so, there were occasions that northerners blew through and Matt's Aunt Geraldine, who'd helped Raine with all the wedding plans, hadn't wanted to brave the chance of having cold or wet guests.

As for Matt, he'd be happy just to find some quiet, out-of-the-way space to park his boots until all the whooping and hollering died down and he could go back to being the general manager of the Sandbur.

"What's the matter, Matt? You look like you're ready to bolt for higher ground!"

The question came from his cousin Lex who'd just strolled off the dance floor after a fast twirl with an energetic redhead. Of all his family members, Lex was probably the most sociable. With his tall blond looks, women flocked to him like snow geese flocked to South Texas in winter.

"It's getting too loud in here," Matt replied in a raised voice so that Lex could hear. "Our new cousins from New Mexico are going to think we're a raucous bunch."

The other man laughed. "We are a bunch of loud Texans, cuz. And from what I can see, our new family members are thoroughly enjoying themselves."

Not more than a month had passed since he'd learned that Raine's mother, Darla, had actually been married to a member of the Ketchum family from New Mexico. Everyone here on the ranch had been shocked to learn they had a boatload of cousins they'd never known about, and for the past few days they had all been getting acquainted. Matt was happy about his new relatives, yet he'd be even happier, he realized, once this shindig was over and quiet returned to the Sandbur.

With a short snort, Matt dug at the tie knotted at his throat. He couldn't remember the last time he'd worn a suit and if he had his way it was going to be a hell of a lot longer before he wore another one. He felt like a green horse that was cinched tight and left to paw with frustration at the saddling post.

"Well, I must be getting old," he commented gruffly. "All this merrymaking is getting on my nerves."

The other man rolled his eyes. "Hell's bells, you're only thirty-nine, Matt. You should be dancing with some of these beautiful women here this afternoon. Who knows, you might get lucky and one of them will seduce you. God knows you'd never take the initiative."

If anyone else had said such a thing to him, he'd give him a mouthful of knuckles. But Lex was like a brother, so he simply glowered at the other man.

"I don't need a woman to dance with—or anything else."

Lex shot him a disgusted look. "Yeah. How many times have I heard that before?"

Fortunately for Matt, another woman, a brunette this time, approached the two of them and wrapped an arm around Lex's. "C'mon, good lookin'," she said to him with a cheeky grin. "You two can talk cattle tomorrow. I've been waiting for a dance!"

Matt watched the pair glide off into a quick two-step, then decided he'd had enough. It wasn't that he was antisocial. He liked people in general. But he'd never been comfortable with merrymaking. Now that his sweet Erica was gone, he wouldn't know how to take another woman into his arms and waltz her around the dance floor. It just wasn't in him.

If he could make it to the kitchen for a cup of coffee, then slip outside without anyone noticing, he could wait out this reception in peace, Matt thought, as he left the loud din in the great room.

Even the hallways and connecting rooms were packed with people gathered together in loose groups while others were simply wandering around with drinks in their hands. He worked his way through the human jumble until he reached the kitchen, only to find it was just as chaotic as the rest of the house.

Scores of servants, most of them hired only for the occasion, were dealing with beverages, food and dirty dishes. He stopped just inside the room and looked around for the familiar face of Cook, the old woman who'd been the ramrod of the Sandbur kitchen for more years than he'd been alive. She was in her seventies now, but she could work rings around a woman half her age. Matt expected to find her slinging hash during this hectic celebration, so it was a surprise to see her seated at a worktable, a cup of coffee clutched in her bony hands.

Well, the old woman must finally be feeling her age, Matt thought, as he made his way over to the cabinet. The idea bothered him. She was like a grandmother to him and all his cousins. He didn't want to imagine the ranch without her.

As he gathered up a cup and filled it from

a huge silver coffee urn, he could hear her saying to someone, "Well now, I never was interested in money. That's not to say I don't like the stuff. Just never had much use for it. I got everything I need right here on the ranch. I don't need to go around digging for treasure. The Saddler and Sanchez families already treat me like a queen."

"I'm sure they do," a younger female voice replied. "But it would be exciting, wouldn't it, if a person did happen to find money buried on the ranch? I've heard the amount might be as high as a million dollars."

His ears wide-open now, Matt slowly stirred a dollop of cream into his coffee while he waited for Cook's response. It came with a snort and he turned around to see she was leaning across the table, her head tilted toward a young woman he'd never seen before. She had light blond hair that was twisted atop her head into a mass of cascading curls. Rhinestones adorned her slender neck and the skinny straps of her dark blue velvet dress. Her skin was shell-pink, her features perfectly etched. Without question, she was a very beautiful woman. Except for her nose, he thought. It appeared to Matt that she was trying to stick it in places where she had no right.

"Bah!" Cook exclaimed with a wave of her hand. "Miss Sara had more money than that before Nate died. But I don't believe she buried any of it. Why would she? It's a silly notion if you ask me."

"Do you know anything about her husband's death?" the blonde asked. "There've been rumors for years—"

"And that's all they are," Matt quickly interrupted as he stepped forward to where the two women were sitting. "Just rumors."

The blonde looked up at him, her pretty rose-colored lips forming a perfect O. Across from her, Cook said, "Matt, this is Miss Juliet Madsen. She works for the newspaper in Goliad. Isn't that somethin'?"

It was something all right, he thought grimly. His eyes narrowed skeptically on the woman's face. "I'm Matt Sanchez, Miss Juliet. And I think you and I need to have a talk. Would you excuse us, Cook?"

"Sure. I need to get back to work anyway," the old cook said.

His eyes still on the nosy guest, Matt placed his hand on Cook's shoulder. "No.

You stay put. Finish your coffee and rest. This won't take long anyway."

Juliet warily rose to her feet and followed the man through the busy kitchen and out the back door. Along the way, her heart was pounding as she eyed the man's long legs, wide expanse of shoulders, and black hair inching over the back of his collar. She'd noticed him before, during the wedding ceremony. Actually, she'd more than noticed. Once she'd spotted him among the grooms-men, she'd hardly been able to observe anything else about the wedding. His hard looks were striking; so much so that just looking at him sent electrical shivers down her spine. Later, she'd learned he was a part of the wedding family, the eldest son of Elizabeth and Mingo Sanchez.

Matt shut the door behind them and Juliet looked around to see they were on a backyard patio that was partially covered with an arbor. Far above the slatted wood and drooping honeysuckle vine, a weak afternoon sun was trying to shove its way through the overcast skies.

Chilly air brushed her exposed skin and she wrapped her arms protectively around herself as she waited for him to speak.

"First of all, I don't know who invited you here," he began, "but that's really beside the point. You—"

"What is the point, Mr. Sanchez?" she quickly interrupted, thinking it would be better to go on the offensive before he took the upper hand. "Geraldine Saddler kindly invited me to the wedding so that I could cover the event for the *Fannin Review*. You find something wrong with that?"

He jammed his hands in his trouser pockets as he stepped toward her and Juliet was glad. He had big hands; the kind that wouldn't let you forget that you'd been touched. Not that he would ever do such a thing to her, but from the furious look on his face, she wasn't sure what might be going through his mind.

"No," he said in a low, smooth voice. "I don't find anything wrong with you taking down wedding details. But that's not what I overheard you discussing with Cook."

Hot color stung her cheeks. So she'd been caught. What could she say that wouldn't make her appear like an indifferent, nosy reporter?

She drew in a bracing breath and let it out.

"I was only chatting with the woman and the rumor as you call it—about the buried treasure on this ranch—just happened to come up."

His nostrils flared like a winded horse and his green eyes narrowed dangerously on Juliet's face. In all her twenty-five years, she had never faced such a man before. She had to fight the urge to race back into the house and run for cover.

"I'm sure the subject just came up out of the blue," he quipped with sarcasm.

She licked her lips and tried not to let her shivers turn violent. "Well, not exactly, but I was just speaking to her about the ranch—off the record, of course."

He took another step toward her and Juliet found her eyes frozen to his hard features: the square jaw, strong, dented chin and chiseled lips that were presently pressed into a tough, menacing line. This man wasn't exactly handsome, she decided, but he was damned sexy. Dangerously so.

"Of course," he said mockingly.

He might as well be touching her, she thought, as she felt his eyes sweep up and down her body. He'd certainly already undressed her with his visual assault.

"Is there anything wrong with talking about the legend of Sara Ketchum's money?"

"Sara Ketchum just happened to be my grandmother. I don't want her memory sullied by some tawdry story in the pages of the *Fannin Review.*"

She tried to look as innocent as possible. After all, she'd not gotten any sort of information out of Cook, and even if she had, Juliet wasn't so sure she would use it. She'd already warned her editor that she didn't like prying into people's personal lives. For one thing, it caused incidents just like this.

"So you think that's what I was doing?" she asked carefully. "Trying to dig up information for the newspaper?"

"What else?"

The woman didn't answer, but there was really no need, Matt decided. She looked guilty as hell. Beautiful, but guilty.

She shrugged one bare, elegant shoulder and he realized with all the skin she was showing in that skimpy dress, she was probably freezing. His eyes skittered once again over the plunging neckline and exposed cleavage of her breasts, then purposely zeroed back on her face. She wasn't dressed all that differently than many of the other female guests roaming around the ranch house, but she damned sure *looked* different, he thought. Her tall, voluptuous figure was enough to send a man's blood pressure skyrocketing.

"Maybe I was just personally interested," she suggested coolly.

Matt snorted. From the sound of her voice, she was from North Texas. She had that certain twang that separated her from the Southern folks of the state. And she wasn't interested in his family; she was interested in her job.

"Where are you from?" he asked bluntly.

Her brows lifted. "Why, I live in Goliad."

Goliad was only about twenty minutes to the east of the Sandbur. He slowly shook his head. "You're not a native around here."

"No. Actually, I'm from Dallas. I moved from there a few months ago when I came to work for the *Fannin Review*."

"Then someone should have told you that the folks down here don't appreciate anyone taking advantage of their hospitality."

She sucked in an outraged breath. "That's not—"

"Don't bother to deny it, Miss Madsen. We both know what you were trying to do and I'm telling you flatly, right now, that there is no story here. And even if there were, I wouldn't let you get anywhere near it. Understand?"

Her nostrils pinched together as she stared angrily at him. "I don't really know what your position is on this ranch, but I've had just about enough of your pious attitude. I haven't committed any crime here. According to a lot of folks in Goliad, it's common knowledge that Nate and Sara Ketchum, the former owners of this ranch had a—well, let's just call it a colorful relationship. And since Nate's murder was never solved, it's still of local interest."

"That's what you think," he quipped.

"No, that's what my editor thinks. He believes the whole issue would make a good story for the paper. I tried to deter him from the idea, but he insisted I ask as many questions as possible." She shook her head in a regretful way. "I'm sorry. I was only trying to hang on to my job."

He glanced away from her pained expression. "Hell of a way to do it."

Juliet bristled all over again. Maybe in his eyes she had been in the wrong, but he could be a little more understanding. Somehow she figured this hard man didn't know the meaning of the word.

"What would you know about needing a job?" she asked. "Looks to me like you were born into riches."

Why was it so easy for outsiders to look around the Sandbur and think that the ranch simply made itself, he wondered. Outsiders could never imagine the long, backbreaking labor that was put into this estate to keep it one of the top cattle ranches in Texas. But then, he couldn't expect this woman to understand. She'd probably spent most of her young life being educated in a private school in Dallas. He seriously doubted she'd ever had those manicured hands in a sink of dirty dishwater.

"You don't exactly look like you've just stepped out of the ghetto, Miss Madsen. But as for me, I've worked for everything I own."

Her chin lifted as she stared at him with angry disbelief. "And you think I haven't?"

His expression turned mocking as his eyes roamed up and down her curvy figure. "I really couldn't say."

Anger propelled her closer and she jabbed a finger in the middle of his chest. "You don't know anything about me. And being some sort of big chief around here doesn't give you the right to be insulting!"

He caught the finger pressing into his chest, then clamped his hand tightly around hers. "Let's not worry about what I am. Let's concentrate on what you are," he growled in a low voice. "You've come to my home under false pretenses—"

"That's not true!" she interrupted hotly, her cheeks burning. "And you have to be the most—hateful bastard I've ever met!"

One corner of his lips sneered upward. "You think so? You think I'm hateful for trying to protect my family from vultures like you?"

"Vul-tt-ture!" she sputtered in outrage. Instant retaliation was the only thing on her mind as she lifted her free hand to slap his jaw.

Matt caught her wrist in midair and then he was gripping both her hands, making it impossible for her to pull away as she stared at him in mute fury.

"You shouldn't have tried that, Miss Madsen," he said in a cunningly smooth voice.

The glitter in his dark green eyes electrified Juliet. Suddenly she couldn't breathe or move the slightest muscle, even when she saw his head descending toward hers.

"Let me go."

The three words were breathed out in a voice so tiny he could barely hear it.

"Why? So you can try to slap me again?" he goaded.

The urge to kick his shin shot through her head, but she didn't have time to carry through with the strike. Before she knew what was happening, he jerked her forward and the front of her body slammed into his.

The contact felt like running straight into a stone wall. The force snapped her head back and made the curls atop her head bounce wildly.

"You—"

The rest of her verbal attack was lost as his lips swooped down on hers. Like a vulnerable little mouse clutched in a hawk's talons, he ravaged her mouth while she stood in a shocked, rigid stance. The heat of his body flowed into her like a sudden arc of electricity and from her head to her toes she felt her skin flushing bright pink.

Just as abruptly as the kiss started it came to a shattering end as he ripped his lips away from hers and set her an arm's length away.

Dazed and gasping for air, she stared at him.

He stared back as his eyes roamed over and over her face.

"Consider that a lesson," he finally said.

His voice was low and husky and Juliet shivered inwardly. The man was more than sexy looking; he was Mr. Sensuality. Too bad he was bent on using his charms in the wrong way.

Quickly, before he could see how stunned she'd been by his kiss, she gathered as much of her senses together as possible and asked coolly, "What sort of lesson would that be?"

"To leave me and my family alone."

His blunt reply was as sharp as a knife. Juliet told herself it didn't really hurt. She'd been spurned before. Yet she felt as if he'd sliced open an old wound and all the times she'd been rejected in the past had come up to slap her in the face.

Drawing up her shoulders, she said, "If the rest of your family is anything like you, it will be a pleasure. Now if I'm excused, Mr. Sanchez, I'm going back inside. It's cold out here and there's no gentleman around to offer me his jacket."

His blood simmering, Matt watched her

turn on a tall, delicate high heel and walk back into the house.

Damn it all, he silently fumed. The newspaperwoman should have never been invited here and for two cents he'd question his Aunt Geraldine about her presence on Sandbur. But since a woman was something he never discussed with anyone, for any reason, he realized he wouldn't take the issue that far. His aunt would think he'd cracked up. Besides, he wanted to push Juliet Madsen totally out of his thoughts. He wanted to forget he'd lost his head and kissed that Dallas woman.

Inside the house Juliet quickly made her way to the restroom and, after locking the door, leaned weakly across the lavatory. A gilded mirror hung over the shallow basin and Juliet was horrified at the image she saw staring back at her.

She looked ghostly pale, except for her lips—and they were almost cherry-red from the hard kiss Matt Sanchez had planted on them. Much of her naturally curly hair had come loose from its pins and several locks were now swinging in front of her eyes.

She'd left her tiny handbag back in the

kitchen under the table where she'd been sitting with the old cook, so she was without a compact, lipstick or comb. Her hands shook as she tried her best to finger comb her tumbled hair back into place and she scolded herself for having such a violent response to the man. It shouldn't matter that he'd taken her unaware with that kiss. She'd been kissed before, she told herself.

But not like that. For a few seconds you were swooning, dreaming of more.

Disgusted with herself, she straightened the straps on her dress, then bravely stepped out of the room and back into the party.

In the great room she was quickly swept onto the dance floor by one man and then another. The music was lively and normally Juliet loved to dance, but as each partner struck up a conversation, she found herself looking around the room, searching for *him*.

Eventually, Juliet decided she'd lost the partying mood and decided to retrieve her purse from the kitchen and head home. She'd already gotten what she'd come for anyway. And more, she thought dismally.

When Juliet entered the kitchen, she found Cook stirring up another bowl of punch. She told the older woman goodbye, then collected her wrap and left the house through the nearest exit. As for thanking Geraldine Saddler for the wedding invitation, she'd do that later through a card in the mail.

Outside the massive, hacienda-style house, the clouds had grown even heavier than when she and Matt were on the patio. The wind was chillier and she gathered the velvet stole higher on her arms as she hurried to her parked car.

Juliet was so intent on getting away from the ranch she almost missed the young girl sitting on one of the half-buried railroad ties that lined the edge of the driveway. She was wearing a long, pale pink dress and her light brown hair flowed in waves down her back. If it weren't for the lost expression on her face, she would have looked totally adorable.

Curious as to why the girl was out here alone, Juliet walked over to her.

"Hello," she said warmly.

The girl, who appeared to be twelve or thirteen, glumly glanced up at her.

"Hi," she mumbled.

"Why aren't you inside enjoying the party?"

Bending her head, the girl plucked absently at her skirt. "Why aren't you?"

Carefully, Juliet sat down next to the girl, while telling herself it didn't matter if creosote stained the seat of her dress. The child emanated sadness, an emotion that Juliet was well acquainted with, and she couldn't leave until she'd found out what was upsetting her.

"Well, I don't really know anyone around here and I'm not all that good at talking to strangers." Or kissing them, either, Juliet thought wryly. "So I decided to head home."

Big brown eyes looked curiously up at Juliet. "I know everyone here today. Except for you. Are you a relative?"

Juliet shook her head. "No. My name is Juliet Madsen and I write stories for the newspaper. I'm going to do one about the wedding."

"Oh." The flicker of curiosity fell from her face and the corners of her lips turned downward. "Then I guess you know my daddy was a groomsman. You probably have all their names down and all that kind of stuff."

"That's right. What's your father's name?"

"Matt Sanchez. I'm Gracia Sanchez and my daddy's the general manager of the Sandbur. Did you know that?"

Juliet didn't know why she was so stunned

to discover that Matt Sanchez had a daughter. The man was probably closer to forty than he was thirty. He'd had plenty of time to acquire a family. But when he'd kissed her—well, she'd never imagined that he had a wife somewhere in the wedding crowd. Dear God, what if the woman had walked in on them? The idea burned Juliet with anger and embarrassment.

"Uh—no. I didn't know that. You must be very proud of him."

The girl shrugged. "I guess so. He's always busy."

The simple statement said volumes and Juliet suddenly remembered her own childhood and a father who'd never been around. No matter if she'd needed him or not. Hugh Madsen's indifference to his daughter's life had left a deep wound inside Juliet, one that had never healed.

Juliet nodded with understanding. "Most men usually are," she said more wistfully than she'd intended, then looked pointedly at Gracia's pink satin dress. "Your dress is beautiful. Did your mother let you pick it out yourself?"

The girl's eyes shadowed over and then she quickly glanced away from Juliet. "I picked it out myself. But I don't have a mother. She died when I was six."

Juliet was suddenly struck with empathy for the girl. Looking at Gracia was like seeing herself twelve years ago.

Gently, she reached over and stroked a strand of gold-brown hair lying on Gracia's shoulder.

"My mother died when I was eight," Juliet told her. "So you don't have to tell me how awful it is. I understand."

Gracia's head twisted back around and she looked at Juliet with surprise. "Your mother died, too? Really? How come?"

Juliet's heart squeezed as faded memories of her ailing mother drifted to the forefront of her thoughts. Eva Madsen had been a softspoken, gentle woman who'd made Juliet's world a magical place with smiles and laughter and a loving hand. When she'd passed away from cancer, Juliet's life had never been the same.

"She was sick for a long time and could never get well."

"Oh. My mother got hurt on a horse and died all of a sudden."

Juliet was suddenly thinking about Matt and how the tragedy must have affected him. He seemed such a stern, unyielding man it was hard to imagine him grieving. But people dealt with personal loss in different ways. For all she knew, the ranch manager might still be mourning his wife's death.

"I'm sorry, Gracia. But sometimes bad things happen to nice people."

She gave Juliet a solemn nod as though she'd already accepted such a fact. "Do you have a stepmom?"

Juliet shook her head. "I only have a father and no brothers or sisters."

A petulant look suddenly stole over the young girl's sweet face. "Me, too. And that's why I don't like being inside today—with the wedding going on. My daddy won't—"

"Gracia! Finally, I've found you!"

Matt's voice interrupted his daughter's words and both girl and woman looked over their shoulders to see him rapidly descending upon them. The cowman's strides were long and purposeful, his expression dour. Juliet felt herself bracing for his presence and when his eyes zeroed in on her face, she unconsciously rose to her feet.

"You! What are you doing out here with my daughter?" he asked sharply.

How could she have had one sympathetic

thought for this man, Juliet wondered. Too bad she hadn't managed to get that slap off. Whacking his jaw would have given her supreme pleasure.

"I'm trying to get to my car and go home."

His jaw tightened. "That's not what it looks like to me."

"You don't know what anything looks like," Juliet shot back.

His gaze settled on her lips and Juliet felt her cheeks fill with unaccustomed heat. Had she actually kissed this man? It seemed impossible and yet all she had to do was look at him and her lips burned with the memory.

"I warned you to stay away from my family, Miss Madsen. And my daughter is definitely off-limits to—"

"Daddy!" Gracia exclaimed as she jumped to her feet and stared at him in horrified embarrassment. "What are you doing? Juliet is my friend and—"

Stepping forward, he placed a hand on his daughter's slender shoulder. "Juliet is not your friend. You don't even know the woman."

The girl shot Juliet a wounded look, then stabbed her father with a tearful gaze.

"Juliet is my friend," she practically shouted.

"And you're being mean and bossy! You never want me to have any friends. Never!"

Jerking away from her father, the girl took off in an awkward run toward the house. It was all Juliet could do not to race after her. The child needed comfort and understanding; two things that she obviously wasn't going to get from this man. But it wasn't her place to give his child solace and he'd be the first one to point that out.

"Feel good now?" Juliet quipped. "Now that you've gotten her away from the evil reporter?"

Matt jerked his gaze off his daughter's retreating back to scowl at Juliet. "Damn it! See what you've done! It's time for pictures and now her face is going to be all red. You're a real piece of work," he gritted.

Forgetting what happened the last time she got close to him, Juliet stepped right in his face. "Your daughter and I were doing just fine until you butted in. But you were so dead set on insulting me that you didn't care whether you hurt and embarrassed her. God, what a cretin you are!"

"If I knew what that meant—"

"It means you have the mental equivalency of an idiot!" she interrupted hotly. "If you haven't looked lately, your daughter is hurting. You ought to focus a little of your time on her instead of worrying about your family's past skeletons!"

Once she'd blasted the words at him, she turned on her heel and began to march in the direction of her car.

Behind her, Matt yelled, "My family doesn't have any skeletons!"

Juliet paused long enough to glance back at him. "Everyone has skeletons, Mr. Sanchez. Even you."

Chapter Two

"I tried, Mr. Gilbert, but Mr. Sanchez practically booted me off the ranch. He made it clear in no uncertain terms that he doesn't want any such stories in the paper about his family. And frankly, sir, I think you'd have a lawsuit on your hands if you did print anything containing the legend of the buried money or the old man's murder." Juliet tried to reason with her boss.

It was Monday morning, two days after the Sandbur wedding, and the editor of the *Fannin Review* was pacing around Juliet's small office like a man possessed. He wasn't happy about her failure to dig up personal information on the ranch's old matriarch and the money she'd supposedly buried to keep from her husband. But then David Gilbert was never happy. Heading toward his sixtieth birthday, he was a frail man with thinning brown hair and a perpetual frown. He'd taken over the reins of the weekly newspaper from his father, who'd died unexpectedly only a few short weeks after he'd retired. From what Juliet could see, he was a man who privately wished he were anywhere but at his job.

"Let him try. Just because that family is probably the richest in Goliad County doesn't mean he can keep the press from public information."

Dear Lord, the man sounded as if he was running some newspaper on Capitol Hill in Washington, instead of a weekly review of small town Texas life, Juliet thought.

Sitting comfortably behind her desk, she tried not to groan out loud with disbelief. "I'm not sure his family's money is public information, Mr. Gilbert. They just might take you to task."

The older man stopped to toss a challenging look her way. "Just let them. I'll be ready. In the meantime, I want you to see what else you can find about the matter. Dig through our old archives, I'm sure there will be something on Nate Ketchum's death. Look through some of the neighboring papers, too. The murder had to have been big news back then."

Any other time, Juliet would have been excited to be working on such a story: love, marriage, money, murder and one of the richest families in the area. Readers loved such things. But in spite of her squaring off with Matt, she'd come away from Raine Ketchum's marriage with the impression that the Saddler and Sanchez families, co-owners of the Sandbur, were nice, genuine people. She didn't want to hurt or anger any of them.

"I'm not sure—"

"You'd better be sure, Madsen. Our distribution numbers have been down this last quarter. We need something to grab people's attention. So I'm giving you two weeks to get something together on this."

"Two weeks!"

Her outcry had him walking over to her desk to stare menacingly down at her. "You don't sound too eager about this, Madsen."

Eager? The whole idea was making her ill. Maybe if this puny little man had to face Matt Sanchez head-on, then he wouldn't be so quick to bark. "Well, I'm just not sure that it's the right thing to do."

His eyebrows shot up as though he couldn't believe she was defying him. "Look, Madsen, you're frankly overqualified for this job. I don't need to pay you a journalist's salary when I could get by with anyone with enough education to structure good sentences. If you don't want to earn your paycheck, then you'd better head on back to the *Dallas Morning News.*"

And face Michael again? Never, Juliet thought. The man had been a cheating lout. He'd broken her heart. She couldn't work in the same room with him. And she couldn't go back and let him tempt her back into his arms. He was no good. Just like the boyfriend she'd had before him. The two guys were a big reason she'd taken this small-time job in an out-of-the-way little town. She wanted to forget all her horrid affairs of the heart.

Glancing away so that he couldn't guess that her teeth were grinding together, she said, "I can do the job, Mr. Gilbert. I'll have something on your desk in two weeks."

"Good. I'll be watching for it."

The editor abruptly left the room and once he was out of sight, Juliet got up and firmly shut the door behind him. Damn man, she silently cursed, he knew as much about running a newspaper as she did about changing the oil in her car, which was practically nothing. The only reason he owned the paper was because he'd been an only child and his father had no one else to leave the business to. Too bad the old man hadn't sold it, Juliet thought grimly.

Well, it wasn't as if she couldn't pick up her belongings and move to some other town and some other job, she told herself. But she didn't want to. These past few months she'd been making friends and settling into a neat little house that she loved. The people were friendly—except for Matt Sanchez—and she liked the slower movement of the small town after rushing around in Dallas all her life. Besides, there was no one who was giving her a reason to live elsewhere. Her father was still in Dallas, but she got more warmth from a stranger on the street than she did from him. Her mother's relatives were scattered throughout the northern states, but she rarely saw or spoke to them. No, she was more or less on her own and she had a right to live where she wanted. And damn Gilbert for threatening her.

Picking up her notes on the Sandbur wedding, Juliet tried to push the whole male race from her mind as she went to work at her computer.

Three hours later, when she broke for lunch, the social piece was finished, all but a few final touches, and she left the building to walk to her favorite restaurant.

The Cattle Call Café was only three blocks away. The red brick building had been built back in the eighteen sixties and was located on the main drag. On the days the livestock auction was being held on the outskirts of town, the café was always jammed with ranchers who'd come to buy or sell cattle and horses. Today the long room, filled with round wooden tables, was only moderately busy with regular townsfolk.

Juliet chose to sit at a wooden bar running along the left side of the room. Almost before her seat hit the red vinyl stool, a young woman with long brown hair and a wide smile waved to her from behind the counter.

"Hi, Juliet! I'll be right with you."

Angie Duncan was a single mother working her way through college. Her shift at the Cattle Call started at eleven in the morning and ended at six in the evening. Juliet didn't know how the woman managed to stay on her feet, much less have a cheery disposition, as well.

"So how's my best friend today?" Angie asked as she approached Juliet.

With a lukewarm smile, Juliet said, "Okay, I suppose."

Angie made a sound of disapproval with her tongue. "Where's that smile I always see on your face? You look like you've just lost your best friend. And that can't be true, 'cause I'm here," she teased.

Juliet tried to laugh, but the sound was garbled. "I'm fine, really, Angie. I just had a long weekend and I'd like to bang an iron skillet over my boss's head."

Laughing quietly, Angie pulled out her order pad. "Okay, tell me what you want for lunch and then you can tell me the rest."

"I'd really like a big greasy cheeseburger with piles of onion rings and a vanilla shake," Juliet told her wryly.

Grinning, Angie tapped a pencil thoughtfully against her chin. "But you're actually going to eat a salad with unsweetened iced tea, right?"

Juliet sighed. "Yeah. Make it a grilled chicken salad."

The waitress left to take the order to the kitchen. While she was gone, Juliet glanced around the café. Other than herself, there were only five people: two older couples and a young man drinking coffee and scanning the daily newspaper out of Victoria.

For some reason Juliet suddenly wondered if Matt Sanchez ever came to town and ate in this café. Probably not. He was from the rich set and the Cattle Call catered to the middle and lower classes of the area. Well, that was all right with her. She didn't want to rub elbows with his sort. And she wished to heck she could quit thinking about the man. But ever since the man had kissed her, she couldn't seem to get her mind back in its regular groove.

The swinging doors to the kitchen swished open and Juliet turned her head to see Angie returning with a tall glass of iced tea. She set it in front of Juliet, then pushed a small container with packets of sweetener toward her.

As Juliet emptied the fake sugar into the tea

and stirred, the waitress propped her upper body on the counter.

"Okay. What's the matter with old Gilbert boy? Been chasing you around the office?"

Juliet groaned. "Lord no! The man doesn't have enough testosterone in his body for those kinds of impulses. I doubt he sleeps in the same bed with his wife."

Angie giggled. "Lucky her."

Juliet took a long sip from her glass. "He wants me to do a story that I don't want to do. And when I more or less told him that I didn't want to do it, he threatened to fire me."

"That's terrible. What sort of story?"

"Something personal about a family around here. He thinks it would grab readers. I think it would cause more trouble than it would be worth."

Thankfully, Angie was prudent enough not to press her for details on the subject. Instead, she asked, "So how did the wedding go? A big deal, huh?"

Sighing heavily, Juliet nodded. "Very big. The house was overflowing with flowers. Real ones. There was live music, lots of food, champagne and dancing. I've never seen so many diamonds and minks in my life."

With her chin resting on her palm, a wistful expression stole over the waitress's face. "Gosh, can you imagine that kind of wedding? That sort of life is a fairy tale to me."

Juliet let out a dry laugh. "Me, too."

Angie waved a dismissive hand at her. "Don't give me that. You're gorgeous. It wouldn't be any problem for you to get a rich man. That is, if you wanted one," she added coyly.

Rolling her eyes, Juliet said, "Well, I've had plenty of trials and errors. I don't want one."

"Juliet! You—"

The waitress was going to say more but the bell at the pickup window rang and she went to fetch Juliet's order. When she returned with the salad, Juliet asked in a casual voice, "Angie, do you know any of the Sanchezes or Saddlers?"

The woman's brows lifted thoughtfully. "No. Not personally. I've seen some of them around before. Mercedes and Nicolette come in here to eat from time to time. So do Lex and Cordero."

The four that Angie had just mentioned were all cousins. Juliet had learned that much at the wedding. She'd also learned the

Sandbur was owned by two sisters, Geraldine Saddler and Elizabeth Sanchez. The latter had passed away and Geraldine was in semi-retirement. It was the two women's grown children that were now seeing after the multimillion dollar ranch.

Thoughtfully, Juliet picked up her fork and stabbed into a morsel of chicken. "But not Matt Sanchez?"

Angie shook her head. "Not on my shift. But that's not surprising. I hear he's something of a hermit."

Juliet had never been one to listen to gossip, but this time she couldn't help herself. "Really?"

"Yeah. That's what a friend of mine who used to work on the Sandbur said. He never saw Matt leave the ranch for anything."

"Oh. Well, I'm sure he's a busy man." Busy insulting women like her, she thought irritably.

"I'd say it has more to do with losing his wife. She died a few years back and everyone says he's never been the same. 'Course, since I didn't know him, that would be hard for me to say. I'm just telling you what I hear." She looked curiously at Juliet. "Why were you asking about him, anyway?"

Why indeed, Juliet wondered. He should be the last thing on her mind. Instead, he was all she could think about. The whole thing was maddening.

"Oh, just curious. He was in the wedding party and he struck me as—well, different from the other men in the family."

Angie gave her a mischievous wink. "Honey, it's his brother, Cordero, that strikes me. He's a hunk and then some."

Juliet looked at her with surprise. "Why, Angie, I've never heard you talk about any man like that."

The waitress shrugged one shoulder. "Well, after Jubal left me to marry the rich girl in town, I thought I'd hate the male race forever. But a woman can't help but be attracted when the right man strolls by."

Shaking her head, Juliet leaned forward so that only Angie could pick up her words. "Look, I've never met Jubal, but I have an inkling he would have never married the rich girl if he'd known you were pregnant with his child. Dear God, I'll never understand why you didn't tell him."

Angie's frown was a picture of disbelief.

"I didn't want him that way! I've told you that before!"

"Yes. But still, he ought to know he has a three-year-old daughter."

Wiping a dishcloth at an invisible spot on the counter, Angie mumbled, "Maybe someday I'll tell him." She looked up at Juliet. "You want anything else? I gotta go warm up the Reynolds' coffee. The old man's looking this way."

"I'm fine. I've got to finish this anyway and get back to work. Gilbert's mad at me enough without adding fuel to the fire."

The waitress went to tend to her other customers and Juliet hurriedly swallowed the last of her salad. While she ate, she scolded herself for giving Angie unwanted advice about Jubal. Juliet was the last person to be giving anyone advice about their love life. Since her days in college, she'd picked some real losers. And the thing that made her choices even worse was that she hadn't realized they were losers until her heart had already been broken.

Bad judgment in men. She might as well have the phrase tattooed on her arm so that she could look down at it every day and remember how much she'd been hurting when she'd fled

Dallas. That memory alone ought to be enough to make her forget about Matt Sanchez and the sizzling kiss he rocked on her lips. But so far nothing was making her forget the heated exchange with the ranch manager.

Two days later, Gilbert gave Juliet the exciting assignment of covering a birthday party at a local nursing home for a resident that was turning a hundred and three. The woman had served many years on the city council and had been a philanthropist in the area, so pictures and a short story in the paper would be expected.

That afternoon, as Juliet drove to the Sunset Manor, she asked herself, as she did many times since leaving the *Dallas Morning News,* if she was wasting herself in this small town with its tiny paper that consisted of mostly local social events. She was a good journalist and she'd written pieces on everything from crime to politics. But the city pace had been exhausting and the pressure to meet deadlines enough to give her stomach problems.

If she could manage to get five minutes of her father's time, he'd tell her it was a hell of a waste to go through years of working and scraping for funds to get herself through college then wind up writing about births, deaths and weddings. But she wouldn't take five minutes of Hugh Madsen's time even if he would give it to her. Just as she'd not taken a dime of his money when she'd been working her way through college.

Hugh was a man that was for one person and one person only. Himself. Even before her mother had died, Juliet could remember him being gone from the house for days on end. There had always been some big deal he was making, the next pile of money to be made. Every now and then he'd hit it big with some new venture, then a few months later be filing bankruptcy.

Even when her mother had become seriously ill, Hugh hadn't changed his high-rolling ways. He'd always made charming promises to his daughter and his wife, but he'd rarely, if ever, come through with them. As far as Juliet was concerned, her mother had died of a broken heart rather than cancer. She'd simply lost her spirit to fight for her life.

At the nursing home, Juliet interviewed the birthday honoree, then took pictures of the woman among her family and friends. The

social room was festooned with bright colored
balloons and strips of twisted crepe paper. A
stereo was providing ballroom music and
several old, but agile couples, were dancing
and holding hands like young lovers. It was a
festive, uplifting scene and as Juliet walked
down the wide corridor of the building, she
felt a little better about the world.

Maybe there was hope for her yet, she
thought wryly. Maybe by the time she grew
to be an old woman she would find the love
of her life.

Juliet was walking along, musing over that
thought, when she passed an open door to a
resident's room. An older man with thick,
dark hair and slumped shoulders was sitting
in a wheelchair and at his feet, a young girl
was reading to him from a small, leather-
bound book.

The girl's voice was sweet and clear and
somehow familiar. Juliet paused in the
corridor for a closer glance and was totally
surprised to see Gracia Sanchez.

For a moment Juliet questioned the
wisdom of making her presence known to
the girl, even if the door was open to the
private room. But the last time she'd seen

Gracia, she'd been crying and fleeing across the lawn. She wanted to make sure the girl had gotten over the embarrassing incident.

Quietly, Juliet stepped to the open door and knocked on the facing. "I'm sorry for interrupting, Gracia. I just happened to see you and I wanted to say hi."

"Juliet!"

Jumping from her seat on the low stool, the girl ran over to Juliet and flung her arms around her waist. Juliet was so surprised by the unexpected display of emotion that for a moment she was at a loss for words.

"I thought I'd never get to see you again!" the girl exclaimed as she stepped back and grabbed Juliet's hand.

Juliet smiled at her. The girl was dressed in blue jeans and a yellow T-shirt with some sort of logo printed across the front. She looked like any normal girl her age rather than the miserable child she'd seen on the front lawn of the ranch.

"Well, I never expected to see you here today," Juliet replied. "Are you visiting a friend or relative?"

Gracia looked fondly over her shoulder at the man in the wheelchair. "That's my grandfather, Mingo Sanchez. He likes for me to read the Bible to him. So I come every other day after school."

It was difficult for Juliet to determine the man's age. His face wasn't that lined with wrinkles, but the twist of his mouth aged his appearance. A wide scar ran from his temple to the back side of his head. Seeing the hairless strip of skin made her wonder if he'd had to undergo some sort of operation.

"That's very nice of you to spend your time with him. Has your grandfather lived here long?"

Gracia tilted her head to one side as she thought about Juliet's question. "Maybe two or three years. I can't remember exactly. He got hurt. Do you want to come in and say hi to him?"

Juliet hesitated. She wasn't all that good with handicapped people and besides that, she had a feeling that if Matt found out she was anywhere near his father, he'd be snorting fire. Still, she didn't want to hurt the girl's feelings.

"All right. Just for a moment."

With her hand still closed around Juliet's, Gracia led her over to the man in the wheelchair.

"Grandpa can't talk, but he understands what you say to him," Gracia explained to Juliet, then spoke to her grandfather in a rapid spate of Spanish.

Once she was finished, the man lifted one hand weakly out toward Juliet. She stepped forward and shook it gently.

"Hello, Mr. Sanchez. My name is Juliet. I'm a friend of your granddaughter's."

He nodded and managed to give her a slow wink. The flirtatious greeting told Juliet the man must be the exact opposite from his son.

Gracia said, "I've already told him about you. I told him about Daddy being rude to you, too."

Embarrassed heat swept across Juliet's face. "Oh. You shouldn't have mentioned that. It's already forgotten." At least, she liked to tell herself *he* was forgotten.

Gracia twirled a strand of hair around her forefinger as she studied Juliet. "Uh—what are you doing here? Do you have family here, too?"

Juliet shook her head. "No. I'm here doing an assignment for the paper."

"Oh. Then you have to go back to work this evening?"

"For a while."

The girl's expression fell flat. "Gee, I was hoping we could go for a soda or something." She glanced at a big watch on her wrist, then added hopefully, "Daddy won't be here to pick me up for another thirty minutes."

Then that meant Juliet had time to be long gone before the man showed up.

"I'm sorry, Gracia, I really need to get back to the office. But if it's okay with your grandfather, why don't you walk with me to my car?"

"Well—it's not like having a soda together," she said halfheartedly. "But it's better than nothing."

In another rush of Spanish, Gracia explained to her grandfather that she would return in a few minutes. Juliet told the older man goodbye and then the two of them left the room.

As they walked down the wide, tiled corridor, Gracia said, "It always makes me sad when I come to visit Grandpa. I want him to get well so he can come home to the ranch. He was my best friend. We rode horses together and he was training a cutter for me so that I could compete. But now—" She broke off with a wistful sigh. "Well—I'm just waiting for him to come home."

Sadness for the girl filled Juliet's heart. "There isn't anyone else on the ranch that could train your horse for you?"

Gracia's head tilted from one shoulder to the other. "Sure, there is. But it wouldn't be the same. My grandpa is the best. He trained champions. It's got to be me and him and Traveler."

"I understand," Juliet replied. "And I'll pray for your grandpa to get well. Sometimes that's the best medicine of all."

Gracia's expression was a mixture of hope and appreciation as she glanced up at Juliet. "That's what Cook says, too. But I don't think my daddy believes prayers will do anything. He goes to mass, but he never smiles when he leaves the church. He's always mad. Guess 'cause Mommy is gone and Grandpa is kinda lost to us, you know."

Juliet didn't know what to say. Hearing Gracia's words had somehow exposed her to Matt Sanchez's pain and she felt as though she'd stepped onto private ground without an invitation.

Resting a hand on Gracia's shoulder, she said gently, "Sometimes it's hard to be happy when things go wrong. That's when we have to have hope that things will get better."

Gracia nodded with adultlike understanding. "That's what I think. I'm going to keep hoping that Grandpa will walk and talk again." She smiled, then abruptly changed the subject. "Do you live here in town?"

The two of them had reached the main entrance of the building and Juliet pushed open the plate glass door and motioned for Gracia to precede her through it.

Once they were outside, Juliet answered, "Yes, I live on the edge of town in a house on Travis Street. It's small and old, but I like it. Maybe you can come see it sometime. If you can get permission," Juliet quickly added. From the bitter remarks Matt had flung at her, she very much doubted he would allow Gracia to visit her, but at least she could let the girl know she was welcome in her home.

"Gee, that would be great. Do you have any pets?"

"A cat. He's a big, fat Persian and he loves attention."

Gracia's brown eyes lit up. "I have a cat, too! Sam's a Siamese with a crooked tail. He loves to catch birds and Cook has been threatening to put a bell around his neck for killing the mockingbirds that eat at the backyard feeder. She hasn't, though. Daddy says it's Sam's born instinct to catch birds and it wouldn't be natural to try to stop him. The big prey on the little, that's what he always says."

Yeah, Juliet thought dourly. And in his case, she just happened to be the little.

Out in the parking lot of the Sunset Manor, several yards away from Juliet's car, Matt Sanchez killed the engine to his truck and reached for the door handle at the same time. As usual, he was in a hurry. A cattle buyer was going to meet him at the Sandbur in less than one hour. He was going to have to break the speed limit to make the meeting in time.

He should have asked Cordero to pick up Gracia. In Matt's opinion, his younger brother didn't visit their father enough. But Mingo would be expecting his eldest son to show up and Matt didn't want to disappoint his father. Short visits from friends and family was all the man had to look forward to.

What the hell?

Matt's hand paused on the door of the truck as his gaze fastened on the woman and girl walking down the steps of the building. It was that Dallas woman with *his* daughter!

What was *she* doing here? And why the hell hadn't she taken heed of the warning to stay away from his family?

Matt's first instinct was to burst out of the truck and interrupt the little tête-à-tête going on between the newspaperwoman and his daughter, but he desperately quelled the urge. Gracia was just now coming round to him after that incident in the yard on the day of the wedding. He didn't want to embarrass her again. Juliet Madsen had been right about that and the fact that he'd been thinking more about his own feelings than his daughter's. It had taken two days of the silent treatment from Gracia to make him admit such a thing to himself, but damned if he would ever apologize to the sexy blonde. She'd probably take pleasure in laughing at him.

Before he knew it, his gaze was traveling up and down her body, appreciating, in spite of himself, the full, luscious curves encased in a black jersey top and a pair of gray slacks. She was not a willowy, fragile woman by any means and he realized her lusty shape did more

than stir the man in him. Each time he laid eyes
on the woman, he felt an instant fire in his
loins. It didn't make sense. Especially since
Erica had died, he'd not even wanted a woman.

But having Juliet against him, even for
those few moments, had burned all sorts of
distracting impressions into his brain. He
could remember the curved indention of her
waist, the full press of her breasts and the soft
skin exposed by the skimpy dress she'd been
wearing. Yet none of those memories were as
strong and dangerous as the kiss of her lips.
Like a blind man with heightened senses, he
had every curve, every scent, every taste
detailed in his mind.

Now after three days had passed, he
realized it had been a grave mistake to have
kissed her. He couldn't forget. And a part of
him didn't want to.

All sorts of mixed feelings raced through
him as he watched Juliet and Gracia
exchange a few more words, then Juliet
leaned down and pressed a swift kiss on
Gracia's cheek. In turn, his daughter gave her
a brief hug, then turned and raced back up the
steps and into the building.

The affectionate exchange hurt him in

ways he didn't want to think about. He'd
tried so hard to be a good father to Gracia.
Especially since she had only one parent.
But it seemed as though the more he tried
to get close, the further she'd drifted away
from him. Maybe it was because she was
going to be turning thirteen next week, he
reasoned with himself. Teenagers couldn't
be figured out.

With the flick of his wrist, he quickly
opened the door and stepped down to the
ground. The movement caught Juliet's attention and she turned where she stood to look
in his direction. For a moment her beauty
stunned him all over again and he swallowed,
a sudden strange thickness in his throat.

He walked over to her.

"Miss Madsen," he greeted curtly.

"Hello, Mr. Sanchez," she said.

"Fancy meeting you here."

Smiling wanly, she reached up and captured
the blond strands of hair being whipped by the
wind. "Yes, it's a small world."

Listening to her twangy drawl was like
warm pudding slipping over his tongue.
Sweet and smooth. "I noticed you just *happened* to run into my daughter."

She drew her shoulders back and his eyes promptly fell to her breasts.

"That's right. I just happened to be here working this afternoon."

His mouth twisted. "I'll bet."

Her eyes narrowed on his chiseled face. "What is that supposed to mean?"

His weight shifted from one boot to the other. "I'm sure you didn't know my father was a resident here," he said with just enough sarcasm to send her brows flying upward.

"Actually, I didn't. I happened to be walking down the hall and saw Gracia."

"I wish I could believe that."

Hefting a camera bag higher onto her shoulder, she turned in the direction of her car. "Believe me, Mr. Sanchez, in spite of your enormous ego, I'm not that interested in you or your family. Tell Gracia it was very nice to see her again."

But not him. She couldn't have spoken the words more clearly. Matt was wondering why that should bother him when she started striding away from him. Before he could stop himself, he marched after her.

"Where are you going?"

As soon as the question popped out of

his mouth he knew it was a mistake. She turned on her heel and shot him a droll look down her nose.

"I do have a job, Mr. Sanchez. I still have work to finish this evening."

So did he. That damned cattle buyer was probably already at the ranch. Why in hell wasn't he worrying about him instead of this sexpot with a tart mouth?

Maybe because she's been on your mind ever since you kissed her.

Shoving that irksome thought away, he said, "I want to know what you think you're doing trying to insert yourself into my family. Particularly, through my daughter."

"Insert? God, you're a sick man. Or maybe I should say fearful. Is that it, Mr. Sanchez? You're actually afraid your daughter might seek out attention from someone other than you? Or do you have something far bigger to worry about?"

His jaw tightened to the point that it was aching, while his hands itched to reach out and grab her. It would give him pleasure, extreme pleasure, to shut her mouth exactly the way he'd shut it three days ago. But this time he wouldn't let himself forget that he was a gentleman. At least, not here in a parking lot where anyone might be watching.

"What are you trying to insinuate?" he countered.

"That you're overreacting for some reason."

He was. And he wasn't exactly sure why. True, he didn't want his grandparents' history plastered about in the paper. But he'd be a fool to think that the locals didn't gossip about his late family. Nate and Sara had been local icons in their era and because so much mystery had swirled around his death and her money, the interest would never die.

Releasing a long breath, he said, "You're right. And if I'm wrong about you, I'm sorry. But then, how could I possibly know I can trust you?"

She gave him a halfhearted grin and Matt could feel his gut tighten at the sight of white teeth against lush pink lips. Everything about her shouted sensuality and he could only wonder what it would be like to have her in his bed, to hear her whimper with pleasure and sigh with contentment.

"You can't know, Mr. Sanchez. Except that I told you I was here on another assignment—you'll read about it in the newspaper.

Also, I met your father. And since his speech is impeded it's pretty obvious I wasn't here to question him."

He looked at her with surprise. "You met Dad?"

She nodded. "Gracia wanted to introduce me and I was glad. Your father seems like a very nice gentleman. I wished we could have visited verbally, I think we would be friends."

No doubt. Mingo had always adored pretty women. From afar that is. As far as Matt knew his father had always been a faithful husband to his wife. But Mingo had never hidden the fact that he liked to look at the opposite sex. Well, he'd certainly gotten an eyeful with Juliet.

"My dad is a nice gentleman," he agreed.

"Gracia is lost without him on the ranch."

It had taken Matt months to realize just how much his daughter was devastated by Mingo's absence on the ranch. Apparently it had only taken Juliet Madsen a few minutes to figure it out.

"I know. But there's not much to be done. He needs a lot of personal care that we couldn't give him at home. We thought about hiring a round-the-clock nurse for him, but one person, especially a woman, couldn't deal with all the lifting and turning. Besides, Dad wants it this way."

She actually looked disappointed and Mingo wondered if she really did feel compassion for his father. It certainly looked that way.

"Is there any hope that he might get better?" she asked.

He shrugged one shoulder much in the same way that Gracia had. "The doctors haven't ruled out all hope, but they're not very encouraging, either. We have more tests scheduled for him in Houston at the end of the month. If we're lucky, something will come out of them."

Juliet nodded. "I hope so. I'll pray for him."

Prayers, he thought bitterly. Who was this woman kidding? For several years after Erica had died, he'd prayed constantly for the rest of his family to be safe and together. In return his father was nearly killed, his strong healthy body reduced to helplessness.

"I have to go. Goodbye, Miss Madsen."

He quickly walked away before either of them could say anything else. Inside the nursing home, he headed straight to his father's room and found the man alone, watching a program on television.

At the sight of his eldest son, Mingo switched off the set and gave Matt a wide smile.

"Hi, Dad. Where's Gracia?"

The man made a motion of lifting something to his mouth and drinking. Matt guessed, "Gone to get you a soda?"

Mingo nodded, then reached for the pad and pencil he always kept in a pocket on his chair. He quickly scribbled two words and handed the paper to his son.

Blond woman.

Matt looked at him. "Yes, Juliet told me that she met you."

Mingo's smile grew broader as his eyes gleamed with pleasure. He then pointed questioningly to his ring finger and Matt knew instantly what was on his father's mind.

"No. She isn't married."

Mingo pointed at Matt, then lifted his fingers to his lips in a kissing motion.

Matt groaned. Dear God, she'd already gotten to his father, too. Where was it all going to end?

Chapter Three

For the next three days Juliet worked on several pieces involving social events and a political issue being squabbled over by the town's council. In between all that, Juliet began to go through the old archives, hunting for anything involving the Sandbur ranch. She'd discovered that the ranch had been a popular news item over the years and as she pieced the bits of information together, she learned far more than she'd ever expected.

As for Gilbert and his idea to print a story about Sara Ketchum's so-called buried treasure, Juliet hated it. These past few days, she'd been hoping against hope that the man would have a change of heart and tell her to drop the whole idea. So far that hadn't happened and as the days began to click by, her mind was spinning faster, searching for a way out.

What was she going to do? Tell Gilbert to kiss her plump behind? She didn't think he'd bat an eye about firing her. In the months she'd worked at the *Fannin Review,* she'd not seen a drop of compassion in him. And no doubt he'd like any excuse to replace her with cheaper labor. She didn't want to lose her job. But she couldn't bring herself to write something about a family that might cause them embarrassment or pain. Not that she was the least bit worried about Matt Sanchez. As far as Juliet was concerned, he could chew on any words she wrote and choke trying to swallow them. But Gracia was a different matter. The child had already been through more than any young person should have to endure. The last thing she needed was to see sordid details about her great-grandparents plastered in the hometown paper.

The telephone on her desk rang, interrupting her dour thoughts. She tried to push them aside as she answered, "Juliet Madsen here."

"Hi, Juliet! This is Gracia. I know I shouldn't call you at work. Can you talk a minute?"

She'd just been thinking about the girl and now here she was on the phone, Juliet thought. Was it some sort of omen? Or was something wrong?

"Sure. Go right ahead."

"Well, I called 'cause I want to invite you to my birthday party tomorrow night. I'm going to be thirteen and Daddy said I could have any sort of party I want, so I'm inviting every friend I have and that means you, too."

Juliet stared thoughtfully down at the papers piled upon her desk. The last thing she wanted to do was disappoint the girl. But the idea of facing Matt Sanchez under any circumstances was a troubling one.

"Is the party going to be at the ranch?" Juliet asked.

"Yes. It's gonna be a barn party. So wear jeans and boots. Cook is gonna fix lots of good things to eat and a giant chocolate cake."

"Sounds like fun," Juliet replied noncommittally.

"Oh, it will be! Say you'll come! I won't have a happy birthday unless you do."

Juliet seriously doubted her lack of attendance would ruin anything about Gracia becoming a teenager, but she didn't say that. Instead, she said, "I'm not sure that would be a good idea, Gracia."

There was a short pause and then, "Why not? Don't you want to come?"

"Of course. It's a big deal to turn thirteen. And I'd like to be there. But your father and I aren't exactly friends and—"

"I've already asked him if I could invite you. He said yes."

After plenty of begging, tears or pouting, Juliet figured. Probably a little of all three. God, she was going to feel awkward, but she couldn't refuse.

"You're sure about that?"

"I'm sure, Juliet. Gee, I wouldn't lie. I'd be grounded for life if Daddy caught me lying."

Juliet couldn't help but smile. At least Matt Sanchez cared enough to teach his daughter morals. Hugh Madsen couldn't have cared less if Juliet told a fib. As long as she stayed out of his hair, he was a happy man.

"Okay. I'll be there. What time?"

"Oh cool! It's at seven. But you can come early and that way I can show Traveler to you before everybody else arrives."

The fact that Gracia considered her a special guest touched Juliet far more than it should have and, in spite of Mr. Sensuous Sanchez, she found herself looking forward to seeing the young girl again. "All right. I'll be there. And thank you for inviting me, Gracia."

The girl gave her a quick goodbye and as Juliet hung up the telephone she wondered what she could possibly take as a gift. What did you give a child that had been raised in a rich family? She didn't appear to be spoiled. Rather, she seemed to simply want attention and affection. The same two things Juliet had always wanted while growing up.

Since Gracia obviously liked horses, the next afternoon Juliet made a trip to a Western wear store in town and purchased the girl a fashion T-shirt with the head of a horse on the front and sequins adorning the neckline and the edge of the sleeves.

After she'd wrapped it in colorful paper and signed a small card to go with it, she dressed in a pair of dark blue jeans and a thin white sweater. She brushed her blond hair smooth before pulling it into a ponytail and fastening it with a white silk scarf. As for makeup, she kept it light. If she were lucky while she was on the Sandbur, she wouldn't meet up with Matt Sanchez. But if she did, she didn't want to give the man any reason to think she'd taken pains to impress him.

Gracia must have been watching for her arrival because as soon as she parked several yards from the house and climbed out of her car, the girl was already there to greet her with a tight hug.

"I should've told you to drive down to the barn where we're having the party," she told Juliet. "I forgot. But we can walk."

Juliet reached back inside the car and pulled out the gift box. Handing it to Gracia, she said, "Happy birthday, sweetie."

Gracia looked at the box in complete wonder. "Gosh, I didn't mean for you to get me a gift. I should have told you that the party wasn't going to be a gift thing."

Smiling impishly, Juliet said, "Well, if you want me to I can take it back."

Gracia quickly shoved the package beneath her armpit and out of the way of

Juliet's extended hand. "Oh no! Since you've already bought it, the polite thing to do is keep it." She rose on tiptoe and kissed Juliet's cheek. "Thank you."

"You're quite welcome."

Looping her arm through Juliet's, she beamed up at her as they began to walk slowly toward the ranch yard and large group of barns and outbuildings.

"Gosh, you look beautiful," the girl told her. "More beautiful than anybody I've ever seen."

Juliet could actually feel herself blushing. "Not really, Gracia. But thank you for the compliment. You're very pretty yourself. I'll bet your mother was a beautiful woman and you took after her."

Gracia's head tilted back and forth as she thought about Juliet's comment. "I remember her being pretty, but I was so little back before she died that now her face just looks sorta blurry when I try to remember it in my mind. I keep a picture of her in my room, though. She had lots of red hair and her skin was really pale. I guess that's why I'm not as dark as Daddy."

So Matt's wife had apparently been white rather than Hispanic, Juliet thought. The fact surprised her a little. He seemed such a straight and narrow traditionalist.

"Mommy was a model, did you know that? She worked in New York and Paris and all those places. But after I was born I think she quit all that."

Juliet was more than surprised by this revelation. She'd not known that Matt Sanchez had been married to a career woman. And she would have never guessed he'd marry a fragile model who made a living off her looks. But love was a strange thing. So far in her young life it had caused her to make several out-of-the-ordinary choices that ultimately turned disastrous.

"She must have loved me, don't you think?" Gracia interrupted Juliet's thought with the question. "To give up a career like that."

Juliet's heart squeezed with an odd little pain. "It sounds like she loved you very much. You should feel happy about that."

She looked up ahead of them to the barn where wide double doors were opened at one end and a stream of workers were coming and going. Juliet gestured toward it. "Is that the party barn?"

Gracia giggled. "That's it. And Daddy says

after tonight's loud music no cow will ever go into it." She giggled again. "But he's only teasing. That barn isn't used for cows."

The man was capable of teasing, Juliet wondered with amazement. She couldn't imagine it. But then maybe she'd only seen the worst in him. At least, she hoped it was the worst.

Once they had walked a fair distance past the big barn, Gracia directed Juliet to a long row of horse stalls that opened beneath a covered walkway. At the third stall, the young girl stopped, then leaned over the half gate and called to the black horse munching alfalfa.

"Come here, Traveler. Come here, boy, and meet my friend."

The black horse seemed to know exactly what Gracia was saying. He walked over to the gate and eagerly thrust his nose at the girl. She pulled two objects that resembled thick, hard cookies from the front pocket on her jeans and allowed the horse to eat them from her palm.

"He goes after those things like I do a chocolate bar," Juliet commented with a soft laugh.

Gracia smiled with deep affection as she stroked the animal's face that had a white streak from his forehead down to his nose.

"Cook makes them out of apples and carrots and oats. All the horses love them, so she makes a whole sackful at a time."

Here on the Sandbur even the animals had a chef, Juliet thought. And Matt Sanchez thought she was spoiled. He didn't have a clue to what her life had really been like. Certainly, it had been nothing like this.

"Traveler's beautiful," Juliet told the girl. "Have you had him for very long?"

Gracia nodded. "He was born here on the ranch. When Traveler was two, Grandpa broke him to ride and, a few months later after he'd learned to rein, he started putting him on cattle. He was learning how to cut real fast. And Grandpa said I was a natural-born rider." Her face grew solemn as she pressed her cheek against the horse's nose. "But then Grandpa got hurt and everything stopped."

Juliet was suddenly remembering the man in the Sunset Manor. One look in his eyes and she'd gotten the impression that he was still a vibrant man trapped inside a useless body. And there was certainly no doubt about the way Gracia felt about him. In fact, it seemed as though she was closer to her grandfather than she was her own father.

"Do you still ride Traveler?" Juliet asked.

Gracia nodded. "Yes. But I just ride him out in the pastures along the cattle trails. I don't try to work with him in the pens."

Juliet didn't know that much about horses or cutting horses for that matter, but she figured when it came to athletic ability they were the same as humans. They needed to learn while they were still young.

"I understand that you want your grandfather to train him," Juliet said tactfully, "but what about your father? Couldn't he work with your horse?"

Frowning, Gracia released her hold on the horse and he moved to the other side of the pen where a few blocks of alfalfa hung in a red, nylon net.

"I wouldn't ask him," she mumbled. "And he wouldn't do it anyway."

Juliet wasn't sure she should ask more. From Gracia's sudden change in attitude, it was obvious she had touched a raw nerve. But she'd gone too far. She had to know why the man with the chiseled face and hard lips would ignore such an important part of his daughter's life.

"Why not?" she asked.

Gracia's chin dipped down to her chest. "'Cause he doesn't like for me to ride. If he had his way, he'd sell Traveler and never let me have another horse. But Uncle Cordero won't let him. He says Daddy is actin' stupid and that someday Grandpa will get well and he'd be mad as hell if he came back home and found Traveler gone."

No doubt, Juliet thought. And it sounded as though Cordero had a totally different outlook on life than his brother's dour, gloom-and-doom attitude.

"Oh. Well, maybe your father will change his mind," Juliet said in the most hopeful way she could manage. "People do have a change of heart sometimes, you know. And besides, it might just be that your grandfather will get his health back one of these days."

A smile slowly spread across Gracia's face and then she took a step over and squeezed her arms around Juliet's waist.

"You're so nice to say that, Juliet. It makes me feel so much better to hear you say it."

Juliet patted Gracia's slender shoulders. "Come on, now. It's your birthday and you're supposed to be celebrating. Let's go over to the barn and we'll look the party scene over before everyone arrives."

Nodding, she grabbed Juliet's hand and led her away from the stables. All the while the two of them walked toward the barn, Juliet found herself glancing around the ranch yard, looking for any glimpse of Matt. But the only men she saw were several cowboys gathered around the tailgate of a pickup truck.

Which was good, she told herself. She'd not come to the party tonight to see the man who'd haunted her thoughts these past several days. She was here for Gracia's sake.

Once they reached the barn, the teenager guided her over to a set of long wooden steps.

"The party is up there?" Juliet asked with surprise as she glanced upward to a square hole in the barn loft floor.

Gracia giggled. "It's got the biggest, nicest floor for dancing. And all the hay has been used—except for a few bales to sit on. Climb on up and I'll follow."

Juliet did as the girl suggested and eventually found herself standing in a long, wide room with open doors on both ends. The wooden planked floor had been swept clean and in one corner tables of food and drink had been set up. Not far away a young man was busy putting together a stereo system. Along with the hay bales, several folding chairs were also positioned around the edges of the room for additional seating. Twisted crepe paper was draped in scallops across the ceiling, while floating balloons were tied to every available post and rafter.

"This is really neat, Gracia. Your friends are going to enjoy themselves tonight."

"I invited some old people, too," she quickly informed Juliet. "Since Daddy said I had to have chaperones, I thought it would be better to have a bunch of them than just one or two. That way they wouldn't get bored."

Juliet laughed. "And just what are you calling old?"

Gracia wrinkled her nose. "Oh, you know. Like Daddy. He's thirty-nine. He's gettin' on up there."

Doing her best not to laugh again, Juliet said, "I wouldn't call him old just yet."

"Well, I'm gonna have the DJ play some country music with the pop, too. That way the ol—uh, the adults might want to dance."

"That's very thoughtful of you, Gracia."

The compliment put a broad smile on the teenager's face and she looped her arm through Juliet's and urged her toward the tables of food. "Come on, I want to show you the neat cake Cook made for me. It's scrumptious!"

While they were looking over the giant chocolate confection, the guests began to arrive and like a good hostess, Gracia excused herself to greet them. Before long, the music was playing and laughter from the young people was filling the loft.

While Gracia enjoyed herself dancing with a young boy dressed in cowboy gear, Juliet retrieved a glass of punch from the refreshment table and took a seat on an out-of-the-way hay bale. She was sipping, tapping her toe to the fast beat of the music when a tall, slender woman with long, brown hair approached her.

"Mind if I share your seat?" she asked.

Juliet recognized her as being the daughter of Geraldine Saddler, but she couldn't remember her first name. She appeared to be somewhere in her thirties and was extremely attractive, even in casual clothing.

"Please do," Juliet told her.

"In case you don't know, I'm Nicolette Saddler, Gracia's aunt," she introduced herself.

Juliet smiled at the other woman. "I remembered you from the wedding the other day being Geraldine's daughter. I'm Juliet Madsen. I write for the *Fannin Review.*"

Nicolette smiled broadly. "Yes. I know. Gracia's announced to everyone that you were coming tonight. You couldn't be mistaken among this crowd," she said with a laugh as she motioned out to the thick crowd of teenagers. She looked at Juliet with a warm expression. "My niece is obviously very taken with you. I'm glad. She needs an adult friend outside of the family. I just hope she isn't pushing unwanted attention on to you."

"Gosh, no. It's nice to have a young person around. Keeps you from being stodgy."

Nicolette smiled again but this time Juliet could see the expression was a sad one. "You're so right. Children keep our hearts young."

"Uh—do you live here on the ranch?" Juliet asked.

The other woman nodded. "With Mother. I moved back about three years ago after my divorce. The house is so big that my brother, Lex, and I never see each other, or our mother, unless we want to. And my younger sister, Mercedes, is away in the air force now, so she's just in and out on rare visits."

Juliet couldn't imagine living such a lifestyle as the Saddlers. She'd been raised in one-and two-bedroom apartments and all of them furnished from resale shops. Her family home had been far from anything to brag about, but while her mother had been alive, the rooms had been full of love. And to Juliet that was all that had mattered. It was later, after her mother was gone, that home had turned into a cluster of cold, empty rooms.

"You have children?" Juliet asked casually.

The sad look returned to the woman's face, making Juliet wish she'd kept her question to herself. Apparently having money hadn't necessarily kept the Saddler or Sanchez families happy.

"No. I haven't been that blessed. What about you?"

Juliet laughed to cover the hollow feeling inside her. "Me? Children? I wouldn't know what to do with them."

Nicolette smiled with disbelief. "You must be doing something right with Gracia."

Shrugging, Juliet said, "That's because she's a special girl."

The other woman sighed. "I'm glad you realize that. She's had too many hurts thrown at her for such a young age. Sometimes I really worry about her."

Juliet would have liked to ask the woman more questions about her niece, but a tall cowboy with blond hair and a toothy grin came up and asked Nicolette to dance, putting an end to the conversation.

Across the room, Matt poured himself a foam cup full of coffee and from a tray of hors d' oeuvres gathered up several fried oysters. He was munching the delicacies, scanning the crowd when he spotted *her.*

He'd known she was going to be here tonight. Still, the sight of her sitting on the hay bale, her blond hair pulled into an innocent ponytail, her unguarded expression strangely vulnerable, was enough to leave him feeling kicked in the gut.

When Gracia had approached him about inviting Juliet Madsen to her birthday party, he'd secretly been shocked. He realized his daughter regarded the woman as a friend, but he'd not realized her feelings toward

Juliet had run deep enough to want her at a family gathering.

And that had irked him to the point that he'd had to fight the urge to give Gracia a loud and definite no. He didn't want the Dallas woman to insert herself into his daughter's life. As far as he was concerned, she could be nothing but a bad influence for a young, impressionable girl. Yet the pleading look in Gracia's eyes had stopped him from expressing his disapproval. At least, that's what he'd been telling himself. He'd allowed Gracia to invite the woman because he'd not wanted to make a big issue of the matter. It was usually true that the more you tried to restrain a child from something or someone, the closer you pushed them toward the taboo.

Maybe that same adage worked with adults, he thought grimly. Maybe if he allowed himself a few minutes with the woman, he'd see for himself that her hair really wasn't as blond and silky, her lips as soft and full, her scent as sweetly seductive as he remembered.

Carrying his food and drink, he slipped around the group of noisy young people and walked up behind her.

"Good evening, Ms. Madsen."

She glanced over her shoulder and he watched her brows lift slightly, her lips part.

"Good evening," she replied.

"Mind if I sit down?"

Her expression skeptical, she regarded him for long moments before she finally said, "Sure. There's enough room here for the two of us."

Matt wasn't exactly sure there was enough room for safety. Yet he couldn't have kept his distance from the woman even if she'd been pointing a gun straight at him.

Walking around to the front of the hay bale, he took a seat a few inches away from her. After placing his nearly empty plate on the floor by his boot, he took a sip of coffee and darted a glance her way. She was staring back at him, her expression faintly questioning.

His gaze fell to her lips and hunger stirred deep in his stomach.

"Uh—I saw the piece in the paper about the Sunset Manor patient," he told her.

A quirk of her lips hinted at sarcasm. "Is that some sort of apology?"

He crossed his legs out in front of him and directed his gaze toward the dusty toes of his black boots. "I wouldn't go that far. It just means I saw the piece and that you were obviously there working."

"Very generous of you."

Normally he would have bristled at such a terse comment, but tonight he let it slide. There were other things on his mind besides putting this woman in her place.

"I'm a little surprised that you came tonight."

She stared at him, mistrust written all over her face. "Why? I wouldn't hurt Gracia by turning down her invitation."

He shrugged one shoulder. "I figured you're a busy woman. And a kid's birthday party wouldn't be your type of thing."

She breathed in deeply, then released it in one heavy rush. "What do you think *my* type of thing is?"

His gaze skittered over her face, then up and down her white sweater. The V-neck teased him with a hint of cleavage and he wondered with a shock what she might do if he reached over and traced his finger under the ribbed edge of fabric until he was touching a breast.

Running a hand around the back of his neck, he forced his gaze up to her face. "Oh, I'd say adult parties would be more your style."

Disdain pursed her lips. "Actually, I don't go to parties. Unless they're a necessary part of my work."

His eyes narrowed. "And what is tonight?"

The flare of her nostrils told him that his question had angered her. But that was nothing new. Everything he said or did seemed to cause her to bristle.

"I'm here tonight as a friend to Gracia. Nothing more. It's an honor to help her celebrate becoming a teenager. It's an important time for her. I hope you realize that."

He sipped his coffee and recognized it had cooled during all this talking. It wasn't like him to be distracted for more than two minutes by a woman and he wondered if something was happening to his body now that he was nearing forty. Maybe his libido was hearing the old clock, warning him that time was ticking by and so was his life.

"I didn't become a father yesterday, Ms. Madsen," he drawled. "I do know a little about raising a child. Do you?"

Hot color suddenly marked her cheeks and throat.

"If you mean do I have any experience raising children, then the answer is no. I haven't had the honor of being a mother yet. And I didn't have any brothers or sisters to care for."

"Then where do you get the idea that you know so much about Gracia?"

She turned her gaze on the group of dancing teenagers and swallowed. "I was her age once, you know. I remember how it feels—how it hurts not to have a mother."

He studied her solemn profile and wondered why he was thinking more about her, rather than his dead wife.

"I suppose Gracia told you all about Erica."

She glanced at him with a stunned expression. "Not really. Only that she was a model and died suddenly when Gracia was six years old."

Leaning forward, he placed his cup on the plate he'd left on the floor. "My wife fell from a horse and it—broke her neck."

His blunt statement shocked her and she stared at him as though he must have said it wrong or that he could somehow change the facts. The idea made him sigh wearily.

"There's no easy way to say it. She shouldn't have been on a horse. She was a fragile, city woman. She didn't know a thing about riding, but she wanted to please me. I guess you could say I killed her. Isn't that what you're thinking?"

Her expression suddenly softened and Matt was shocked at how much he wanted to reach over and touch her hand, to feel the female contact he'd avoided for so many years.

"I'm thinking," she said softly, "that an accident happened. And it was just meant to be. That's all."

He let out a long breath, then nodded briefly. "Yeah. Just meant to be," he quietly echoed.

Juliet's mind was spinning, wondering what she could possibly say to him next when a pair of jeans-clad legs and lug-soled boots suddenly came to a screeching halt in front of them.

She looked up to see Gracia smiling broadly at the two of them.

"Hi, Daddy! How do ya like the party? Neat, huh?"

Reaching up with one hand, he patted her cheek. "Very nice, honey. Are you enjoying yourself?"

"Yeah! This is great! All my friends are here. Especially Juliet!" With a perplexed frown, she tilted her head and studied her father. "Why don't you dance with her, Daddy? That would be the polite thing to do."

He looked at his daughter dumbly, then finally said, "That's not my kind of music, Gracia."

The teenager giggled. "I can fix that. I'll go tell the DJ to play something just for you!"

Before Matt could protest, Gracia had taken off at a run to the table where the young man hired for the evening was spinning records and CDs. In a matter of seconds, the pop song ended and a slow country ballad filled the loft.

From across the room, Gracia waved happily to them and Juliet looked helplessly at Matt. "I think your daughter wants us to dance."

One corner of his lips curved into a semblance of a smile and he rose to his feet and offered his hand down to her.

"Then we'd better not disappoint her. After all, you said this was a special night for her."

Juliet was so shocked she wondered if she should pinch herself to make sure she wasn't dreaming. But the moment she placed her hand in Matt's, the sizzle along her palm told her she was very much awake and the man drawing his arm around her waist was all too real.

"You'll have to forgive me if I step on your toes. I haven't done this sort of thing in—a long time," he said as he began to slowly move her around the floor.

"Don't worry. I won't yelp very loud if you smash one or two," she said.

He actually smiled at that and Juliet felt her insides turn as gooey as chocolate pudding. The man was lethal without even trying, she thought helplessly.

"And I'll just bet you can get loud—if you want to," he remarked.

The sway of their bodies and the warm change in his attitude was lulling her, urging her to think of him as just any man. But he wasn't just any man. He was Matt Sanchez, the manager of this multimillion dollar ranch, and the widower of a beautiful model. Juliet didn't fit in with a man like him, but for the next few minutes she could dream.

"I guess you've already figured out that I'm opinionated, but I don't get loud—unless someone makes me really mad," she added with a little laugh.

"Hmm. Guess I haven't made you *really* mad yet. I haven't heard any yelling from you."

How could a woman yell when she was being kissed, Juliet thought wryly.

They danced a few more steps in silence and then he said, "A while ago you said something about not having a mother. Is your mother deceased?"

Juliet nodded. "She passed away from cancer when I was eight—that's why I understand some of the things Gracia feels."

After a moment, he said, "I see."

Dear Lord, but it was something to have this man touching her, Juliet thought languidly. To have his hard chest brushing against her breasts, his strong legs moving next to hers. She wanted to move closer, to wrap her arms around his neck and see if his kiss was as wild and delicious as she remembered.

"Do you really?" she asked.

"I'm a cowboy. Not a total dunce."

I'm a cowboy. With those three words he'd described himself perfectly. He had that wild, free cowboy spirit. That Wyatt Earp, shoot-'em-down swagger that would intimidate almost any man that got in his way. And as for the women, she could only wonder how helpless one would be if he should set his sights on her.

She sighed. "Gracia is a wonderful child. You should be very proud of her."

"I am." He looked down at her. "But I'm worried about her."

His green eyes were darker than a field of alfalfa, she thought, and the lines fanning out from the corners only seemed to make him sexier. She realized her heart was thumping out of control and had been from the moment he'd taken her into his arms. She tried to tell it to calm itself. This was only a dance and a few civil words with the man, nothing to get excited about.

"Why?" she asked.

"I'm worried about this affection she's placing on you. I don't want her to get attached and then have you leave her."

Juliet thought about Gilbert's threat to fire her if she didn't write the piece about Matt's grandparents. The problem was not a minor one, but for tonight, she wasn't going to allow herself to dwell on it.

Tilting her head back, she looked at him with resolution. "I'm not going anywhere. Goliad is my home now."

His brief smile was a picture of doubt. "You say that now. But eventually Dallas will call you back."

She frowned at him. "Why would you think that?"

"Because you're here to get away from something back there."

How could he possibly know that, she wondered. Could he see her shattered ego or had he tasted it in her kiss? In any case, it irked her that he thought he knew so much about her.

Deliberately evading his comment, she said, "I'll be here. Whenever Gracia needs me, I'll be here."

He suddenly stopped the dance and she looked at him, slightly dazed.

"What's the matter?"

An amused grin touched the corners of his lips. "The song has stopped. And since it's already played three times, I figure everyone else is tired of it."

Shocked that she hadn't noticed, Juliet glanced around them to see that, other than the two of them, no one else was on the dance floor. The idea that everyone had been watching them make intimate circles around the room was enough to splash bright pink color across her cheeks.

"Why didn't you stop before now?" she asked in dismay.

"Because I thought I needed the practice," he answered with a sly little grin.

Practice? The man was as smooth as glass, she thought, and more dangerous than one of those Brahman bulls he raised. Angry or charming, he had enough presence to almost, almost make her forget her vow to never fall in love again.

Chapter Four

Once they reached the edge of the dance floor, Matt dropped his hand away from Juliet's back and inclined his head toward a group of adults standing near the refreshment table.

"I see an old friend I need to speak to," he told her. "Thank you for the dance."

"You're welcome," she murmured.

He walked away and Juliet felt a long breath of air slowly pouring from her lungs. Being in the man's arms had shaken her badly and she told herself she was glad he'd moved on to another guest. She needed to smooth her ruffled senses and remind herself that he was off-limits. Way off-limits.

She was making her way back to the hay bale where she'd first been sitting when a cowboy near her age approached her for a dance. At first she started to politely decline, but at the last moment decided to accept the man's offer. After all, she didn't want to seem unfriendly to any of the folks here on the Sandbur and besides, dancing with another man might help her get her mind off the complex ranch manager.

The dance turned out to be one of many as several other male guests invited her to take a spin on the dance floor. Juliet visited with each of them and truly tried to keep her attention focused on what each one had to say, but in the back of her mind, she kept thinking about the way Matt had touched her, the words he'd said to her. Just being near him excited her in ways she'd never felt before and made her other dance partners pale in comparison.

Nearly an hour passed before she found herself alone again. By then she was thirsty and damp with sweat from the exertion of stomping out several Texas two-steps. At the refreshment table, she poured herself a glass of fruit punch then took herself to a spot in the room that was empty and a bit quieter.

She was sipping her drink with one hand and fanning her face with the other when Matt slipped up beside her.

The sight of him startled her. While she'd circled the dance floor, she'd covertly searched for him in the fringe of crowd. She'd not spotted him anywhere and had decided he'd left the party to the younger people. Apparently he'd been nearby the whole time.

"You've been busy," he said with a wry quirk to his lips.

Her heart fluttered and she forced herself to glance away from his face. "I've never believed in being a wallflower."

The lines around his mouth deepened with something like amusement. "I'm sure you were never one of those," he said, suddenly raising his voice to be heard above the music.

The DJ had decided to give the young people a treat and the sound of a pop tune was now rattling off the barn rafters. As Gracia and her friends crowded onto the dance floor to enjoy themselves, Matt stepped closer and curled his fingers around her upper arm.

"This is killing my ears," he mouthed close to her ear. "Want to go down and get some fresh air?"

Was he serious? She looked at him, but his expression was too smooth to read anything. His motives weren't the real issue. Juliet knew to spend one minute alone with this man in the moonlight was as dangerous as dancing around a rattlesnake. Still, she was too charmed and too curious to refuse the invitation.

"All right. It would be nice to cool off a bit," she agreed.

With his hand at her back, the two of them made their way to the end of the room where the wooden ladder would take them to the ground. Matt allowed her to go first and when she was safely at the bottom, she stood to one side and waited for him to descend.

Once he reached her side, she commented, "The night is beautiful. I'm surprised there're no kids down here running around."

"It's because of the rule," he explained. "Gracia made it clear to all the kids she invited that once they go up, they aren't allowed to come down until the party is over and everyone is going home. There're too many dangers around a ranch to have young people running loose. Especially when some of them are just itching to get into mischief."

Juliet nodded. "You're probably right. And it would be awful for Gracia's birthday party to be marred with an accident."

"Yeah. There've been enough of them around this ranch already."

She didn't know if he was talking about his wife's accident in particular or other incidents. Maybe he even considered the death of his grandfather an accident. Yet from what Juliet had researched on the subject, all evidence pointed to a cold-blooded murder committed by someone who'd been an enemy to Nate Ketchum. But she didn't want to think about that story now or Gilbert's demand that she write about it.

Matt reached for her arm and turned her away from the entrance of the barn. "Let's walk," he suggested.

He took her on a path that led to the shed row where Gracia's horse was stalled. The night air was mild enough to make her comfortable in her sweater. The sky was clear and stretched a carpet of stars for as far as the eye could see. As they ambled away from the loud music in the barn, she could hear cows bawling softly in the distance and a breeze tinkling the leaves of a nearby cottonwood. She tried to concentrate on the soothing sounds rather than the hot sizzle Matt's hand was sending throughout her arm.

With his free hand he gestured to the area to the left of them. "That's the holding pens over there. That's where we put the cattle when we're getting ready to ship them out." He motioned to the shed row just up ahead. "And that's where we keep a few of our horses stalled. Usually the ones that are in training for cutting or reining."

"Gracia brought me out here earlier to show me her horse, Traveler," Juliet told him. "He's gorgeous."

He let out a heavy breath. "She's fixated on that damn horse," he said with frustration. "I've tried getting her interested in other things like ballet lessons, piano, violin, soccer, but she won't have any of it. If she had things her way, she'd spend all of her spare time with him."

There were always two sides to everything, Juliet thought, and she was hearing Matt's now. "It's not unusual for a young girl to be horse crazy," she told him. "Plenty of them are. I was that way, even though I didn't have a horse. I constantly dreamed of having one and competing in the show ring. I think it's a healthy interest. But I can see you don't."

He glanced at her sharply. "No. I don't think it's healthy. In fact, horses are extremely dangerous. Every time she gets on Traveler, all I can see is Erica lying lifeless in the dirt. It's not something I want to live over and over every day."

His wife had been dead for several years now, but it was obvious that even now he was dealing with her death. Apparently he was still carrying love in his heart for the woman and that idea made Juliet very uncomfortable. For one thing, she envied the late Erica Sanchez for having this man love her that much. For another, the idea that this tough man walking along beside her could feel that much, hurt that much, made him far more appealing than she wanted to admit.

They walked along in silence for a few moments and Juliet realized the very masculine scent of him was competing with the dirt and hay and livestock around them. For one brief moment she closed her eyes and breathed deeply.

"You ride, don't you, Matt? And I'm sure your brother and cousins do, too. I'd even bet that your Aunt Geraldine still climbs in the saddle."

"We men ride out of necessity, Juliet. As for Aunt Geraldine, she's an excellent horse-woman. I don't have to worry about her."

Juliet glanced at him as she said tactfully, "Well, Gracia will be an excellent horse-woman, too, with practice."

"Hmph. You have an answer for every-thing, don't you?"

Why did she want to cuddle herself against his side? Why did she want to feel his arms around her, when she knew he could be nothing but a heartbreaker to her? Was she destined to be attracted to men who would ul-timately hurt her?

"Not really. I just know that Gracia needs you. She needs your attention and admiration."

Incredulous, he paused to look at her. "She told you this?"

Careful now, she said, "Not in so many words. It's just obvious that—she adores you and wants you to be proud of her."

The tense line of his shoulders relaxed and he shook his head with wonder. "It wouldn't be possible for me to be more proud of her than I already am. She's growing into a beautiful girl. And she's very bright and ambitious. She's in the top five percent of her class. I don't have to push her to study or do her chores. I couldn't ask for a better daughter."

She gave him a lopsided smile. "But you would ask that she give up her horse—the most important thing to her?"

His lips formed a grim line as he urged her forward. "I'm not demanding that she give up Traveler. Even though I'd like to," he admitted.

Thank goodness he understood his daughter that much, Juliet thought. With a sigh, she said, "I'm sorry if it sounds like I'm trying to tell you how to raise Gracia. I'm not—I just want to make sure you understand her from a—woman's perspective."

"You mean a mother's viewpoint, don't you?"

By now they had reached the long line of stables, all of which were protected by a deep overhang lit with dim night-lights. As the two of them stopped beneath the shelter, Juliet turned to study his shadowed face.

"I can't pretend to know what a mother knows," she confessed.

He studied her face for a long moment, then with a hard swallow he looked away from her toward the horse hanging its head over the stall gate.

"I might be a lot of things, Juliet, but I'm not a blind man. I can see that my daughter needs a mother. And I wish I could give her one. But I have no desire to get married again. I doubt I ever will."

His admission didn't surprise Juliet, but it did sadden her. Even if he didn't have Gracia to consider, the man needed love, she thought. If he was so all knowing, why couldn't he see that?

"Why? Would it make you feel guilty if you loved a woman other than your late wife?"

He dropped his hand away from her arm and Juliet fully expected him to blast her with some angry retort. Instead he quietly turned the tables on her.

"Before I answer that, don't you think it's time you told me about your love life? You're a beautiful woman. I'm sure you've had marriage proposals. Why aren't you married, or have you been?"

Until that moment, Juliet hadn't realized just how much the broken relationships in her life had shadowed her spirit, her belief in herself as a woman. Her last boyfriend, Michael Hamlin, had been a regular charlatan. But unfortunately she'd not figured that out until later. Almost too late, she thought grimly. He'd given her an engagement ring and their wedding had been set to take place. She'd been filling a new apartment with things to set up housekeeping with her new husband, and in her mind, she was picturing them with children and years of togetherness. But then she'd gotten the call from a so-called friend hinting that Michael might not be all he seemed to be. Juliet hadn't wanted to believe the caller, but the seed of suspicion had been planted and she'd begun to take a second look at her fiancé. She'd discovered he not only had a present girlfriend, but that he'd had a string of them while professing his love to Juliet. To say the least, her hopes and visions of being a happily married woman had ended then and there.

"I've never been married," she said in a low voice. "I came close once, but that didn't work out. So far men have disappointed me and to be honest, I just don't think I could ever trust one enough for marriage."

He frowned. "That sounds pretty jaded. Especially from a woman as young as you."

"Twenty-five doesn't feel that young to me." Suddenly feeling awkward, she stepped around him and over to the horse.

He followed her, but didn't say anything and after a moment Juliet realized he was waiting for her to say more. But she didn't want to say more. She didn't want this man to know that every man she'd ever had in her life had wound up treating her badly. It didn't speak well for her judgment or her ability to make a man love her.

Reaching out gently, she stroked the horse's nose. "My father was—is a real bastard, Matt. For as long as I can remember, he treated my mother horribly. There were other women and then there were these get-rich-quick schemes that usually ended up in bankruptcy. He was always making glorious promises to her and ninety percent of the time they were broken. When I was a child and didn't know any better, I thought he was just one of those men that had bad luck. I believed he was really trying to make a good home for us and I believed he really loved Mother and me. Even though he hardly ever gave me a passing glance," she added bitterly. "Funny how children think a parent is automatically supposed to love their child. I did. Until I learned better. Now I figure I'm much happier living alone than—being in that sort of misery."

Her views on love and marriage were no concern of his, Matt thought. And he shouldn't have asked her in the first place. The only reason he had was because she'd seemed so dead set to pry into his intimate life. But now that she was talking, he was listening, and the pain he heard in her voice touched him far more than he wanted to admit.

Stepping closer, he reached out and touched a strand of golden hair lying upon her shoulder. It felt soft and cool and even without bending closer, he could smell the scent of flowers upon it.

"You've told me your mother passed away," he said quietly. "What happened between you and your father after that?"

Her hand paused upon the horse's face. "Oh, at first, for a couple of years he made an attempt at raising me. But it didn't work.

He resented being tied down and he didn't have time for a kid. I cramped his style and he didn't mind telling me so. Thankfully, my mother's sister only lived a few blocks away and I would run to her house for comfort. Until eventually, I quit running and just stayed there until I was old enough to get out on my own."

Matt didn't know what to say. He'd not expected her to come from such a difficult background. The first time he'd met her, he'd gotten the impression that she'd been born into an easy life where two parents had coddled and spoiled their darling daughter. Then he'd learned her mother had died while Juliet was only a small child and now he'd heard her father was not fit to be a parent. He felt awful that he'd misjudged that part of her life so badly.

"I'm sorry, Juliet. I really am."

In the muted light, she turned to face him and even though she tilted her chin proudly he could see pain in her eyes. The sight struck him deep within his chest.

"You don't have to be sorry, Matt. I don't worry about what Hugh Madsen thinks of me now, or even if he ever thinks of me."

Her face was so brave, yet so sad and beautiful that he couldn't stop his hands from capturing her shoulders and pulling her toward him. She came into his arms without resisting and as her full, luscious body settled against his, a fire ignited low in his belly.

With her face against his shoulder, he stroked her hair and her back, all the while knowing he should set her away, but loving the feel of her too much to follow the commands of his cautious side.

Moments passed as her body heated his and then her head stirred and he turned his cheek close to hers. Their breath mingled and then she let out a helpless groan.

"Matt, I—"

"Don't talk."

Juliet had to obey his command. She had no other choice as his lips quickly covered hers and his hands drew her even closer to his hard body. She'd not expected him to be touching her like this or kissing her again, and the shock of it momentarily stunned her with questions. But as his mouth began to move hungrily over hers, the whys quickly fled her mind. She couldn't wonder what was going on in his head. All she could do was experience the exquisite taste of his hard lips.

With the speed of an arrow, desire plunged through her body and before she realized exactly what she was doing, her mouth opened and her arms slipped around his neck. She wanted to be closer. Had to be closer.

The silent invitation lured his tongue deep inside her mouth and the intimate connection made the hidden spot between her thighs ache with need. Another moan rattled deep in her throat.

Without breaking the kiss, he walked her backward, into the shadows, until her shoulders came in contact with the wall of the barn. The privacy of the darkness seemed to fuel his desire even more and she refused to think or to question when his lips pulled away from hers to make a hasty descent down the neckline of her sweater.

Like raindrops of fire, he scattered kisses over her skin until his mouth settled in the valley between her breasts and then his teeth began to nibble, his hands moved to the rounded fullness of her bottom. Roughly, he tugged her hips against his and she could feel the bulge of his desire pushing against his jeans, against her.

Wanting, needing to feel all of him, she pulled his hat from his head and dropped it to the ground before her fingers slipped into his black, silky hair. With the pads of her fingertips pressed against his skull, she urged his mouth to the tip of one breast, then moaned as he bit through the thin fabric of her sweater until his teeth found her nipple.

His name was a silent plea upon her tongue and she was just about to whisper it, to beg him to make love to her when suddenly the sound of people talking and laughing in the distance drifted to them on the breeze.

Jerking his head up, Matt hurriedly glanced over his shoulder.

"Some of the guests are leaving. We'd better get back."

His voice was thick and husky, telling Juliet he'd been just as lost in the moment as she. The idea was frightening. Yet she didn't want to go, to leave the passion of his arms.

Unable to speak, she simply nodded. He stepped back from her and bent down to retrieve his hat from the ground. The parting of their bodies allowed cool sanity to slip back to her senses and she suddenly felt like an idiot for behaving so wantonly. He could have made love to her without even asking and the embarrassing part was that they both knew it.

"I—uh—it's time for me to go home," she blurted, then stepping around him, took off in a brisk walk toward the house.

Juliet was past the barn and almost to the spot where she'd parked her car when Matt caught up to her and she shivered outwardly as he captured her by the hand and spun her around to face him.

"You're going without saying goodbye? Gracia will be hurt," he said.

What about him, she wanted to ask, would he be hurt? But she'd already exposed her attraction to the man; it wouldn't do to let him think there were feelings behind her kisses.

She stared at the ground. "Please tell her goodbye for me and that I had to leave early. I'll—call her later and thank her for the lovely party."

He didn't respond immediately and when he spoke again she was bracing herself, expecting him to accuse her of trying to seduce him.

"You don't have to leave because I stepped out of line, Juliet."

Surprise brought her gaze up to his face and as she stared at his lips heat began to sting her face. The ache of desire still lingered in her body and she wanted to step forward and into his arms. She wanted to complete the ecstasy he'd started in the shadows.

"You didn't—" She broke off as he stepped closer.

"Yes, I did," he countered, his voice raspy and full of self-reproach. "I don't know what you're thinking right now—but I didn't plan any of that, Juliet. I—hell—" He looked away from her, toward the lights of the nearby ranch house. "I haven't wanted any woman since Erica died. But you—" Drawing in a deep breath, he turned a troubled gaze back on her. "You're very beautiful, Juliet. And sexy. And I guess the man in me hasn't died yet. I wish—you'd just forget the whole thing ever happened."

His awkward apology stunned Juliet and somehow drew her to him just that much more. Yet she could see that he obviously regretted their heated embrace for one reason or another and wanted to make sure she knew it would never be repeated. A wise plan for both of them, she realized. Yet the idea left her feeling very empty.

"Sometimes things happen that—well, just consider the whole thing already forgotten, Matt," she said gently.

Nodding soberly, he dropped his hold on her hand and Juliet felt the chill of the night breeze.

"Yeah. Things just happen," he murmured.

His gaze was still on her face and she wondered how she could tear her eyes away from him, but somehow she managed to say good-night and turn and walk briskly to her car.

Five days later, Matt was still trying to forget Juliet and the reckless way he'd behaved with her the night of Gracia's birthday party. Since then he'd not seen nor spoken to the woman, yet her image had hounded his brain until he could hardly think of anything else.

He was staring off into space, reliving the way she'd tasted, the way her body had molded to his when his cousin Lex's voice broke into his erotic thoughts. The two men had been riding since just after dawn, search-ing a pasture on the far reaches of the

Sandbur for newborn calves. The day had been long and tiresome. Even the dogs trailing behind the horse's heels were ready to get home and have their supper.

"Matt? Are you listening? I asked if you wanted to ride through the deep end of the river or go down to Settler's Bend where it's shallow?"

With a tired sigh, he looked over at his cousin, who was covered in trail dust. "Let's swim the horses," Matt told him. "I don't want to ride another thirty minutes and I'm sure the horses don't, either."

Lex nodded. "I'm game. A little cold water won't hurt us. In fact, it might wake you up."

Matt frowned at him. "Wake me? I haven't been asleep."

"Maybe not. But you've been doing a hell of a lot of daydreaming. It's a good thing we brought the dogs with us today, otherwise I wouldn't have had any help at all."

"Like hell," Matt shot at him. "You wouldn't have found a third of those calves if I hadn't been with you."

Lex snorted good-naturedly. "All right, I'll concede you've been working, but your mind is somewhere other than here." He glanced thoughtfully at Matt. "Are you—worried about something? Gracia giving you trouble?"

Worried? Annoyed was much more like it, Matt thought. It was downright irritating to have his mind taken over by a female with long legs and an hourglass figure.

Picking up a corner of the yellow kerchief tied around his neck, he used it to wipe the sweat from his face. "No. I'm not worried about anything," Matt told him. "And Gracia hasn't given me an ounce of trouble." Except that the sight of his daughter always reminded him even more of the blond vixen from Dallas, he thought wryly.

"Well, you've been preoccupied with something these past few days." Lex's eyes narrowed as he studied his cousin's weary profile. "If I didn't know better, I'd think you've been daydreaming about Ms. Madsen."

Shocked that Lex would bring up Juliet's name, he turned a glare on the other man. "Why the hell would you say that?"

Lex shrugged. "Just a hunch. Ever since you whirled the woman around the dance floor, you haven't been acting like yourself."

That much was true, Matt thought, but he didn't necessarily want to admit it out loud, or to his well-meaning cousin. "There's nothing wrong with me. Just because I'm trying to do some quiet thinking—"

"About what?" Lex interrupted. "Long blond hair and an even longer pair of legs?"

Matt's back teeth gnashed together. "The nicest thing you could do for me right now, Lex Saddler, would be to shut up."

Lex chuckled. "Damn, Matt, why do you want to raise your bristles at me? I think it's pretty great that you've finally taken a look at another female. And for your information, so does Nicci."

Matt had to fight like crazy to keep from groaning loudly. If taking a look at Juliet was his only crime, he probably wouldn't be feeling so possessed right now. Lord, what would Lex and Nicci think if they knew he'd nearly made love to the woman?

Closing his eyes, he reached up and wiped a hand over his gritty face, in hopes it would wipe the images of those moments with Juliet out of his mind. But nothing seemed to help dim the memories of that night. He could still taste and smell her, feel the curves of her breasts in his palms, her hips pressed to his. If those partygoers hadn't interrupted them, he would have soon had her lying out on the grass. The need he'd felt for her had been so hot it was still enough to make him shudder.

"Look, Lex, there's nothing going on with Juliet and me. She's Gracia's friend and I was—only being hospitable."

Lex laughed loudly and Matt couldn't blame him. He'd sounded lame and they both knew it.

"C'mon, cuz, it won't break your neck if you admit you're attracted to the woman."

"It might break yours if you keep this up," Matt retorted.

Laughing again, Lex glanced at him as their mounts picked their way forward through the tall sage grass, wesatch and clumps of prickly pear.

"You're not eighty years old, Matt, and I don't believe you feel like it, either."

"You don't have a clue how I feel," Matt muttered glumly.

Lex's laughing features took on a sober look. "No. I haven't loved a wife and lost her. But seven years have passed since Erica died. It's time you woke up and looked around. And I'd be damn happy if Juliet Madsen could finally open your eyes."

She'd opened his eyes all right, Matt thought, and now he was seeing clearly. The Dallas woman was all wrong for him. It didn't matter that her kisses set him on fire or that she was the most beautiful, sexy woman he'd ever seen. It made no difference that her smile, her laugh, made the corners of his mouth want to turn up and the heaviness in his heart seem just a little lighter. She was a born-and-bred city woman. Maybe she wasn't as fragile or out of place as Erica had been in his world, but she was still from a different life than his. Even if Matt wanted her to, she wouldn't fit in. And then he'd lose her.

"My eyes *are* open, Lex. And what I see up ahead is the river. We'd better put our stirrups up and get ready for a cold swim." And hopefully the chilly water would break this fever Juliet had given him, Matt thought desperately.

He spurred his horse toward the banks of the San Antonio.

Chapter Five

The spring morning had started out sunny with no hint of a cloud in sight, but by the time Juliet left her office for lunch the sky was gray and a steady rain was wetting the streets.

Since she was only a couple of blocks from the Cattle Call Café, she dug out an umbrella she kept for just such emergencies and walked the short distance.

By the time she reached the diner, wind had spotted her skirt with raindrops and her sandaled feet were wet. Before she stepped through the doorway of the busy café, she shook the umbrella and her pleated skirt, then shook back her loose hair that was curling wildly from the damp air.

Today the bar was full, so she found a small table with two chairs at the back of the room. She settled herself in a chair nearest the window and, as she waited for Angie to come take her order, glanced around the busy room.

Today was obviously sale day at the local county livestock barn. The diner was full of ranchers both young and old and the sound of male conversations and gruff laughter filled the café. As Juliet's gaze scanned the crowd of eaters, she looked for Matt or a familiar face from the Sandbur, but she found none. Of course, it was probably foolish to think he or any of the men from the big ranch would be attending such a small livestock sale. The Sandbur was in a different league than most of the local ranchers. They didn't sell just a small herd at a time. They shipped out tractor semi-trailer loads of cattle to buyers in far-off places.

"Sorry, Juliet. I know you've been waiting, but this place is crazy today. I'm surprised you found a seat."

Juliet looked around to see a harried Angie standing near the edge of the table. Black smudges of fatigue were under the young waitress's eyes and her normally shiny hair was dull and pulled back into a nondescript bun.

"Don't worry about me, Angie. I have plenty of time. Just give me a taco salad and a glass of iced tea."

Angie began to scribble on her pad. "I missed you these past couple of days. Have you been sick?"

"No. I've been eating a sack lunch at my desk, but today I decided I needed to treat myself to something other than a can of tuna and a carton of yogurt. What about you?"

The other woman let out a weary breath. "I'm okay. I'll tell you about it later. Right now I'd better put your order in and start making the rounds with the coffeepot. These men have already guzzled about a gallon of the stuff."

Juliet shot her a heartening smile. "Maybe you'll get a bunch of good tips."

Angie groaned with misgivings. "I hope you're right. God knows I need them."

The waitress hurried away and Juliet picked up a newspaper that someone had left on the corner of the table. It was the daily issue from the neighboring city of Victoria and she began to scan the articles in spite of her practice to avoid any kind of reading on her lunch break. She needed something to concentrate on other than the dark cowboy from the Sandbur. But even articles about troubled politicians and local immigrant smuggling weren't enough to draw her thoughts away from Matt.

Darn the man. Why had he ever invited her to take that walk with him in the first place? If she'd stayed in the barn, where she should have stayed, she wouldn't be sitting here looking for him, wondering what he was doing, or if he'd thought about her since their tryst at the shed row.

Somehow she doubted their heated exchange in the shadows had affected him nearly as much as it had her. After all, a man didn't need much urging when he had a female body in his arms. Nor did he need much motive to seek pleasure where it was so readily offered. She'd been handy and the moment had been right, that's all there was to the matter, she reasoned with herself.

Yet these past few days Matt's awkward apology kept going round and round in her mind—*I haven't wanted any woman since Erica died. But you—* What had that meant?

That she was special? No. She couldn't let herself start thinking in that direction. Matt had more or less told her that he had no interest in finding love with any woman. And Juliet had vowed over and over not to let herself get involved with another man—especially one who had issues longer than her grocery list.

She was staring out the window at the falling rain, trying not to think about the man when a vaguely familiar voice sounded just behind her.

Glancing over her shoulder, she was more than surprised to see Matt's cousin, Nicolette Saddler, dressed in a slim peach-colored suit and a pair of high heels. The woman was definitely a class act, Juliet thought.

"Ms. Saddler, how nice to see you!"

She smiled and extended her hand to Juliet. "It's Nicci, please. And I don't mean to interrupt your lunch. In fact, I'm on my way out. I just happened to see you when you entered the café and I thought I'd come over and say hello."

Smiling, Juliet shook the woman's hand. "I'm glad. Are you sure you don't have time to sit down and have a cup of coffee or something else?" she invited.

Her expression regretful, the pretty brunette

shook her head. "Sorry. I'd love to, but I'm on my way to work. And since I've already taken off this morning, I'm going to pay dearly this afternoon."

Curious, Juliet asked, "Where do you work? At the ranch?"

Nicolette let out a brief laugh. "No. I've done my share of ranch work in the past, but I have a safer job nowadays. I'm a physician's assistant at a health clinic in Victoria."

Juliet looked at her with wide eyes. "A doctor! I'm impressed."

Nicolette gave her a modest smile. "Not really a doctor. Just close to one," she corrected, then her expression took on a definite twinkle. "I thought I'd better warn you that you have the whole family abuzz."

Turning slightly, so that she would be facing the other woman, Juliet looked at her with surprise. "Abuzz? I'm sorry—have I—done something wrong?"

Matt's cousin chuckled freely this time and Juliet realized it was the first time she'd ever seen the woman with a genuine look of pleasure on her face.

"No. Not at all. In fact, we're wondering how you managed to do something right."

Confused, Juliet shook her head. "I'm afraid I've lost you."

"Matt," the other woman explained. "You got him out on the dance floor the other night. That was a complete miracle. And all the family is beholden to you. We've been trying to get him to—well—come back to life, so to speak. But with Matt it's like trying to reason with a wall of stone. When Lex and I saw him dancing with you it really made our hearts glad. You see, he's been so lonely and bitter for such a long time. And someone like you is just what he needs."

Except that he doesn't want someone like me, Juliet thought. At least not for more than five minutes.

Dropping her gaze to the tabletop, she said quietly, "Thank you for saying that, Nicci. But it was just a dance. Matt has his own ideas about what he needs and I don't think it's a woman. Certainly not me."

The doctor's face turned thoughtful as she studied Juliet's bent head. "Would you like to be his woman?"

Shocked by such the direct question, Juliet's head jerked up. "Are you serious?" she asked in a stunned whisper.

A gentle smile crossed Nicolette's face. "I'm sorry for being so forward. Sometimes I forget that asking personal questions doesn't always work outside the examining room." She shrugged and began again. "But actually, I was serious. I just get the feeling that you're attracted to Matt and I wanted to tell you not to give up on him. He's worth fighting for."

Amazed by this whole conversation, Juliet could only wonder what this woman would think if she knew that Matt had nearly made love to her. Would she be happy about that, too, or would she see Juliet in an entirely different light. Like a woman from the wrong side of the tracks looking for a nice little meal ticket.

"Look, Nicci, your cousin is an extremely sexy man. I'd have to be frigid not to feel some attraction for him. But he's—well, I'll just be frank, he's a walking heartache. And since I've had plenty of those already, I'm not too eager to jump into any sort of relationship."

The woman's face went suddenly sober and she nodded perceptively. "I understand what you're saying, Juliet. And I apologize for sticking my nose where it doesn't belong. I just happen to like you. And I think Matt likes you, too."

A corner of Juliet's lips curved upward. "The feeling is mutual, Nicci. On both counts."

With a brief smile, the woman reached over and gently squeezed Juliet's shoulder. "I hope we can visit again sometime."

Juliet nodded. "I'd like that."

As the woman turned to leave, Angie glided up to the table with Juliet's lunch. The waitress cast a curious glance at Nicolette Saddler's back before she placed the taco salad in front of her friend.

"That was Ms. Saddler—the doctor from the Sandbur," she whispered as she leaned toward Juliet. "What was she doing over here at your table?"

Juliet's lips curved with amusement. It would never occur to her friend that she was being just a bit nosy.

"Just saying hello."

Angie's eyes widened. "Really? You know *her?*"

The waitress made it sound as though Nicolette was royalty and Juliet supposed to the people around Goliad the Saddler and Sanchez families were the closest thing to monarchs. Their generations had settled this area and over the years they'd built an empire. As with most wealthy people they were envied, admired and sometimes hated.

"Slightly," Juliet admitted. "I met her at a party I attended the other night at the Sandbur."

In spite of the café being packed, Angie sank into the chair opposite Juliet's and leaned eagerly toward her. "Why haven't you told me about this? You, at a party on the Sandbur! How did you ever get invited? Or was it work for the newspaper?"

Juliet wasn't one to talk about her personal life. Yet she knew that Angie was lonely and hungry for any kind of socializing, even the secondhand kind.

Picking up her fork, she stabbed into the lettuce and spicy meat piled upon the fried tortilla shell. "It had nothing to do with work. Matt Sanchez's daughter, Gracia, invited me. It was her birthday party. She was turning thirteen."

Angie looked even more confused and Juliet explained. "I met Gracia at the wedding and we became friends."

"Oh. Gosh, rubbing elbows with the elite, what's that like?"

Juliet stifled the urge to groan. She'd done

far more than rub elbows with one member of the ranching royalty. She'd come close to making love to him. God, what a mistake that would have been, when just kissing her had seemed to riddle him with guilt and regret.

"They're just regular folks like us, Angie. They just happen to have more money in the bank than we do."

The sparkle of excitement that had been in Angie's eyes was now replaced with a dull look of worry.

"They wouldn't have to have much to outdo me," she said glumly. "I don't have any money in the bank. Mine goes as quickly as I get it."

"Don't feel badly. Most of us live that way." She picked up her tea and took a long drink before she asked, "Angie, I don't mean to sound critical, but you look terrible today. Are you feeling okay?"

Sighing, the waitress leaned back in the chair, then took a quick glance around the room to make sure no new customers had strolled into the café. "I'm all right. Just exhausted. Melanie has been sick for the past two days with a fever. I've been sitting up at night bathing her with cool cloths. During the day while I'm at work, the babysitter has been tending to her. We give her fever reducer as much as we can, but it keeps coming back."

"Oh, I'm sorry. What does the doctor say is wrong?"

The worrisome frown on Angie's face deepened. "I get my paycheck today so I'm going to take her to the doctor this afternoon."

"Angie! Why have you waited? If it's money—"

"Juliet, there's no doctor around here that will see a patient on credit. They all want to be paid right then, Johnny-on-the-spot. Besides, even if I'd taken her earlier, I wouldn't have had money for medicine."

"There're programs for assistance, Angie. You need help and—"

Shaking her head, Angie interrupted. "I'd have to give up my job to get benefits. I'm not going to do that, Juliet. I don't want handouts so—Melanie and me just fall through the cracks."

The bell over the café door jingled as another pair of customers stepped through the door. Seeing them, Angie rose tiredly to her feet. "I gotta go. I've already sat here too long."

Juliet thoughtfully watched the young

woman hurry away. Angie's three-year-old daughter was an adorable child. She could hardly bear to think of her being ill and not getting the medical attention she needed. Yet Juliet understood completely what it was like to be so penniless that it was all a person could do just to keep shelter over her head and food on the table. Once she'd left the haven of her aunt's home, she'd not taken a penny from anyone, especially her shiftless father, who sometimes had money and often-times not. Like Angie, she'd worked at waiting tables and all sorts of odd jobs to pay the rent and tuition for college. The only dif-ference being that Juliet had only had herself to be responsible for. It was difficult to imagine going through those tough times with a child at her side.

If only there was a doctor around who'd be willing to help Angie and her daughter, a doctor who wasn't in the business just solely for the money, Juliet thought as she munched through her salad.

Nicolette Saddler. The physician's assis-tant suddenly popped into Juliet's mind and as she thought about the gentle woman, she couldn't imagine her turning away an ill patient over money. Especially a child. If she knew the clinic where Nicolette worked, Juliet would take it upon herself to call the woman. But she didn't have a clue and a city as big as Victoria had many medical facilities. Of course she could call Matt and ask him. But she didn't think he would appreciate the intrusion. After the night of the party, she figured she would never hear from him again.

Well, that left Nicolette's mother, Geraldine. She was slightly acquainted with the woman. Perhaps she could explain the situation with Angie to the Sandbur matriarch and see how things went from there. At least it would be a try.

Finishing off the last bites of her salad, she took a couple of twenties from her handbag and left them by her plate. Angie would find them later and probably be angry with her, but Juliet would deal with that when the time came. Right now she wanted to help a friend.

Later that evening in the Sanchez house, Matt had just sat down to the evening meal with his daughter when she turned a pleading smile on him.

"Daddy, I was thinking it would be nice if we could have a picnic this weekend."

The piece of steak on the end of his fork stopped halfway to his mouth. "A picnic. We've never done that sort of thing before."

Her big hazel eyes were impish and sparkling, a big improvement from the cheerless gaze his daughter usually gave him. He wanted to think it was the concentrated effort he'd made this past week to be with her at the supper table every evening. But a part of him figured Juliet Madsen had a lot to do with it. Since Gracia had become friends with the woman, she'd slowly started coming out of the sad shell that had surrounded her for months now.

"That's more reason why we should," Gracia reasoned. "You work too hard, Daddy, and I hardly ever get to see you."

He popped the piece of rib eye into his mouth and chewed slowly. "We've been spending every evening together," he reminded her.

She nodded. "I know. And it's nice not to be sitting here alone or with Uncle Cordero. But I want us to do things—together."

Gracia needs you. She needs your attention and your admiration.

Juliet's words marched through his mind and warned him to choose his next words carefully.

"And you want us to have a picnic," he reiterated.

She put down her fork and looked at him with excitement. "Yes! We could ride our horses down to the river where it's shallow. And if it's warm we could even go wading."

With a slight shake of his head, Matt said, "Gracia, your dad is too old to do such things. That's for young people, like you."

She pursed her lips. "Well, it wouldn't be too old for Juliet. I know she'll like it. If you don't want to wade, you can stay on the bank and eat."

Matt sat up straighter in his chair. "Whoa, now. What's this about Juliet? I thought you were talking about the two of us."

She turned another imploring look on him and Matt wondered how females were born with the innate ability to know exactly when to turn on the charm.

"I was. But I thought it would be really cool if Juliet could go with us," Gracia answered in a rush. "She knows how to ride—she told me so. And it would be neat to have the two of you with me. It would be—"

She broke off awkwardly and Matt watched her thoughtfully as she twirled a long strand of hair around her finger.

"Go on, Gracia. It would be what?" he prodded.

Bending her head, she studied her plate for long moments, then finally she looked up at him, her expression both daring and hopeful. "Well, it would be almost like having a real family with me."

Something stabbed him deep in the gut, but he tried to ignore the pain. He didn't want his daughter to see that she'd rammed a thorn in his side.

"You mean like a mother and father," he said quietly.

Her head suddenly bobbed up and down with the relief that he understood. "Yeah. Like that."

He drew in a deep breath and let it out. "Well, Gracia, you need to remember that Juliet is not your mother. And she won't ever be."

Horrified, the teenager stared at him as if he'd just spoken blasphemy and then she blasted out at him. "My mother is gone! She won't ever come back! And Juliet won't ever be my mother because of you! Because you're too mean and you don't understand anything but those stupid cows and—and—"

Tears strangled off the rest of her words as she jumped from the table and raced from the room.

Matt rose slightly from his chair with intentions of going after her, but after a moment's consideration he eased back down in his seat. It would probably be best for both of them if he allowed her enough time to calm down before he tried to reason with her.

Several rooms away, he heard a door slam loudly and realized the noise was a result of his daughter leaving the house. More than likely she was heading up to her Aunt Geraldine's house where she could find a little female solace.

His sigh was heavier than a ten-pound brick as he stared down at his half-eaten steak. So much for spending quality time with his daughter, he thought miserably. He'd made an utter mess of things. But what the hell was he supposed to do, just give in and give his daughter anything she wished for, he asked himself.

Groaning with frustration, he rose from the table and stalked to the library where a small wet bar cordoned off one corner of the room. After he'd filled a squatty tumbler with chunks of ice and a stiff amount of Kentucky bourbon, he carried the drink to his bedroom.

There he sank into an easy chair positioned in front of double windows that ran from ceiling to floor. With the drapes pulled he could see the western skyline, but tonight the evening star was blotted out by the remnants of a rainstorm that had passed through earlier that day. The night was black and lonely, just like his heart.

Ice tinkled against glass as he dourly lifted the drink to his lips and downed half the contents. He wasn't a drinker. Never had been. But tonight Gracia's outburst had left his nerves as prickly as a cocklebur and he needed something to soothe him before he had to face her again.

My mother is gone! She won't ever come back!

As his daughter's words rolled around in his head, he took another long sip of the bourbon and grimaced as a trail of fire traveled from his throat to his gut.

Juliet won't ever be my mother because of you!

Gracia had never spoken to him with such anger or disrespect before and he should have been angry with her. Very angry. Instead, all he could feel was worry and loss and frustration. It was plain she needed and wanted a mother. But he was in no position to give her one. And his daughter was going to have to learn that love and marriage was something that just didn't happen because a person wanted it to.

Chapter Six

Juliet placed the old newspaper on the floor beside the sofa and closed her burning eyes. She'd been reading for hours now, stories that had been published down through the years about Matt's grandparents, Nate and Sarah Ketchum. From what she could gather, the couple had lived a colorful, if sometimes difficult, life together. And she had to agree with Gilbert that a story about the king and queen of the Sandbur would pique reader interest. The couple made for fascinating reading. But she wasn't prepared to do a story about the two of them. Not when she knew it would end anything there might be between her and Matt. Not to mention the devastation it might cause Gracia, particularly at school where peers could be judgmental.

So what was she going to do about writing the article, Juliet asked herself for the thousandth time. Gilbert was making noises, wanting to see the progress she'd made toward the story. So far the only thing she'd managed to do was pull up old archives and write a few notes. But that wasn't going to satisfy the editor for much longer. He'd threatened to sack her if she didn't come through with a scandalous article about the Ketchum's and the so-called buried money. So that left her stuck at the edge of a cliff with no way out but down.

With a weary sigh, she pushed herself off the couch and headed toward the tiny kitchen in her small house. A cup of coffee might help her think. At the least, it would help her stay awake so that she could read for another couple of hours.

She'd assembled the water and coffee grounds and was flipping the switch on the coffeemaker when the telephone on the corner of the cabinet rang.

Juliet hoped it was Angie with news about Melanie's fever. She was worried about the little girl.

"Hello."

"Is this Juliet?"

Matt's voice stunned her for a moment and she stared at the countertop as her mind raced through flashbacks of the party and their stroll through the night. She was certain she'd never hear from him again.

"Yes."

"This is Matt."

Gripping the receiver, she swallowed hard and tried to make her voice light. "Yes. I— recognized your voice. How are you?"

There was a long pause before he finally answered, "Okay."

The terse reply told her nothing about the reason for his call and she blew out a long expectant breath as she waited for him to further explain.

"Are you busy?"

His question vaulted her mind to the stack of papers in the living room, papers with pictures and articles about his grandparents. What would he say if he knew she'd been reading them? Juliet shuddered to think of his reaction.

"Uh—no. Actually, I was just making myself a cup of coffee."

"Oh." That's what he should be drinking, Matt thought, instead of something to dull his senses. If he had, he might not be on the telephone now, making a fool of himself. "Well, I don't mean to interrupt, but I—I'm calling to see if you have anything planned for Saturday."

"Saturday?"

She said it as if she'd never heard of such a day of the week and Matt realized this whole phone call had taken the woman by surprise. But hell, he'd shocked himself even more when he'd looked up her number and punched it through.

"Yes. Are you busy this coming Saturday?"

"No. I don't think so. Why?"

The drawl of her voice wound through him like a ribbon of warm pleasure. Closing his eyes, he could see her face, her lips and smell that elusive scent of flowers on her skin. Wanting her was something he still didn't know how to deal with.

"I—that is—Gracia and I—were wondering if you'd like to go riding with us. We might take a lunch down to the river. That is—if the weather is nice."

"A picnic? Really?"

He grimaced. "You sound doubtful. Don't you think I know how to have a picnic?"

A nervous little laugh sounded back at him. "Not exactly. You don't seem the type. And I'm sure you're making this invitation for Gracia's sake."

"I'm making it, that's all that matters," he said a little gruffly.

"Does that mean you actually want me to accept? Or that you just want to be able to tell Gracia you did your part?"

He swiped a heavy hand through his black hair. "Why are you making this so hard? You either want to come or you don't."

She didn't say anything for a long moment and then she spoke in a low voice, "I'm not sure I should, Matt. After the other night— it's obvious you don't want to get tangled up with me. And—"

"You assured me that you'd forget about— what happened between us. Now you're bringing it up. I—"

"All right, I told you I'd forget, but I simply can't wipe it from my mind. I've tried. And a woman is a curious creature, Matt. I'd like to know, at least, what's behind this invitation."

So she hadn't been able to forget any better than he had, Matt thought grimly. He didn't know whether that news pleased or worried him. "Nothing is behind it, Juliet. Gracia likes your company and—so do I. It's just a damn picnic," he added irritably. "Nothing more."

"Okay. I accept. When should I be there?"

She didn't sound all that excited about the prospect, but that part of it didn't matter. She'd accepted; he couldn't ask for more.

"Ten should be early enough. Come to the Sanchez house. We'll go from here."

She agreed and then before he could make any sort of reply, gave him a quick goodbye. After the phone clicked dead in his ear, Matt hung up the receiver and left the bedroom. It was getting late and he wanted to make sure Gracia had returned to the house.

The den, where Gracia usually worked on her homework or watched television was empty so he made a quick detour to the kitchen just in case she'd decided to eat. It was a cinch that she ought to be hungry. When she'd fled from the supper table, her plate had been full.

He found Juan in the kitchen. The old Mexican was watching a Texas Rangers' baseball game on a small TV perched on the end of a cabinet counter. The old wrangler had become the cook for the Sanchez household a little over a year ago when the young woman who'd held the job had married and moved from the area. Juan had once been one of the best wranglers on the Sandbur. He could rope a cow with his eyes closed and horses that had once been labeled outlaws had been tamed by his gentle hand. But he was now in his seventies and a fall from his horse while gathering cattle had severely broken his hip. The joint had to be replaced and Matt had given the job of cook to the man to make his recuperation easier.

Juan spared a glance at Matt and because the old man spoke only broken English he rattled the question in Spanish, "Has Gracia been in here?"

Juan answered in his native language.

"All right. If she shows up hungry, fix her something to eat. She didn't eat her supper."

His expression grim with disapproval, the old man nodded. *"Si."*

Turning on his heel, Matt left the kitchen and headed up the staircase to where the bedrooms were located. There was a chance that Gracia had climbed the stairs and entered her room without him hearing.

When he spotted the slit of light coming from beneath her door, relief washed through him. In spite of everything, Gracia was the light of his life. She was the reason he worked from dawn to dusk to keep the ranch prosperous. He wanted her life to be good and he wasn't about to depend on some future husband to provide for her. He wanted her to have a legacy and dependable security, long after her father was gone.

Drawing in a bracing breath, he knocked lightly on her bedroom door.

"Gracia?"

When there was no response, Matt pushed the door open and stepped into the dimly lit bedroom. The space reflected his daughter's tomboyish taste. Instead of ruffles and lace and a canopy bed, she had plain pine furnishings, dark corded curtains and a matching comforter. Books were piled everywhere, along with a few CDs of her favorite music. There were no stacks of stuffed animals, dolls kept over from her younger years or posters of pop idols on her walls. Instead, there were endless photos of horses and her grandfather,

Mingo, holding many of the cutting trophies he'd won over the years.

On a tall chest near the bed stood a framed picture of Gracia's mother and Matt could only wonder if his daughter would look different, be different if Erica were still alive.

Sighing quietly, he stepped farther into his daughter's private space.

She was lying crosswise on the double bed, her cheek pressed against the comforter. Her long hair had slid forward to hide most of her face, but Matt knew without seeing her expression that she was aware of his presence. Her thin little body was more than still, it was tense with anticipation, like a yearling colt just haltered for the first time.

"Gracia?"

She rose to a sitting position and looked at him with faint defiance. "I guess you're here to punish me," she said, her voice raw with emotion.

Pain squeezed his heart like a heavy hand. He'd always wanted his daughter to have fighting spirit, and with Sanchez blood in her veins, she'd come by it naturally. He didn't want to squash that spirit or hurt her in any way, but it seemed as though he was always upsetting her.

"No. I'm not here to punish you. Even though I'm not happy with your disrespectful behavior."

Her head bent as she nervously plucked at the comforter. "I'm sorry," she said glumly. "I—shouldn't have said those things to you."

Maybe she should have, Matt thought miserably. At least her outburst had gotten him to thinking about more than the calf spring tally.

Easing gently down beside her, he picked up her hand and pressed it between the two of his.

She raised her head and looked at him with misty eyes and in that moment he realized how very much he wanted to please her, to understand her.

"I have something to tell you," he said.

Surprise and confusion crossed her face. "You do? What?"

He suddenly felt very awkward. "I—uh—called Juliet a little while ago."

Her eyes widened with disbelief. "You did? You actually *called* her?"

Nodding, he rose from the bed and began to move around the room. "She's agreed to go with us on a picnic Saturday. So it looks as though we'll be going—unless the weather is bad."

She didn't immediately reply and he was about to turn around to see her reaction when he was suddenly smacked from behind and two little arms snaked around his waist and squeezed hard.

"Thank you, Daddy! Thank you! This is the coolest, greatest thing you've ever done for me!"

Amazed, Matt inwardly shook his head. Offering her several hundred dollars to go shopping wouldn't have garnered this joyous reaction from her.

Unwrapping her tight hold on him, he turned and placed a kiss on the top of her head. "I'm glad you're happy, but before you start getting too carried away, just remember that this is a picnic with a friend. Nothing more. Okay?"

With a broad smile, she snuggled her cheek against his midsection. "Anything you say, Daddy."

It's only a picnic.

Saturday morning Juliet was repeating those words to herself as she pulled to a stop in front of the Sanchez ranch house, but she couldn't quite make herself believe them.

There was nothing simple about spending time with Matt Sanchez, especially when the time was intended rather than by chance.

After plucking a small handbag, along with a light jacket from the passenger seat, Juliet climbed out of the car and started up a narrow brick walkway that led to the tall, two-story house. As she walked along the path, she took a closer look at the red brick structure built in typical plantation style. Huge white pillars supported the second-floor balcony, which also provided a portico for the bottom floor of the house. White wooden shutters, which could actually be opened and closed, were fastened on either side of the many long windows adorning the front.

It was a beautiful structure, but entirely different from the hacienda-style home where Matt's cousins resided. In fact, this Grecian-style home was far different than anything in the whole area and she wondered how it had come to be.

Up ahead a wide wooden door with a gold knocker opened and Gracia stepped out dressed in jeans and boots and a long-sleeved

T-shirt. The moment she spotted Juliet, she waved and raced toward her.

"Hi, Juliet! Are you ready to go?" she asked excitedly.

As ready as she'd ever be, Juliet thought wryly. To Gracia, she said, "I think so. What about you?"

"I need to get my things from the house. Want to come in? Daddy is getting the horses ready. He'll be here in a minute."

The child whirled back to the house and Juliet followed her quick steps onto the wide planked porch and into a large foyer filled with potted palms. Along one wall, on a deacon's bench were a brown cowboy hat, a jean jacket and a bottle of water. Gracia scooped up the pile of things and turned a happy smile on Juliet.

"Can you believe it, Juliet? Daddy is actually going riding with me!"

Apparently this was something out of the ordinary, Juliet thought. Especially when she remembered Matt telling her that he hated the sight of Gracia on a horse.

She smiled at the teenager. "I'm glad. Maybe this will give him a change of heart about your riding."

Gracia's cheeks dimpled impishly as she glanced at Juliet. "I think he's already had a change of heart. Thanks to you."

Juliet was about to correct her on that score when the door suddenly opened and Matt stepped into the foyer. He was dressed in jeans and boots and a plaid shirt of greens and blues. A black cowboy hat was pulled down low on his forehead, but she didn't have any trouble seeing his eyes. They instantly latched onto hers and she stared while heat danced colorful footsteps across her cheeks.

"There you two are," he said. "Hello, Juliet."

She stepped forward to greet him and though her first instinct was to rise on tiptoe and kiss his cheek, she pushed the notion out of her head and thrust her hand out to him. "Good morning, Matt."

Slipping off a leather glove, he took her hand and held it.

"I'm glad you could come."

One corner of his lips curved into a faint grin and Juliet decided the expression was as sexy as the calloused skin of his hand against hers.

"I'm glad I could make it," she replied.

"I have the horses ready to go." His fingers tightened perceptibly around hers as his gaze swept over her jeans and boots and thin, gray sweater. "Did you bring a hat?"

Juliet shook her head. "I'm afraid I don't have one. But I won't need—"

She broke off as he turned a pointed look to Gracia. "Go get her one of yours, honey."

He'd barely gotten the order past his lips when Gracia turned on her boot heel and hurried out of the foyer. "I'll be right back!" she called to them over her shoulder.

Once Gracia had disappeared, he looked down at her as he continued to hold her hand. "Gracia's excited about this. I think I am, too."

Juliet was staggered by his comment, but she tried not to show it. Matt was a complex man and she decided it would be best not to read too much into anything he said or did. Not if she wanted to keep her heart and her sanity.

"I'm glad. I just hope I haven't forgotten all my riding skills."

His brown eyes continued to sweep over her face. "I've saddled you a docile mount. All you have to do is tell him when to go and when to stop. He'll do the rest."

She could feel his eyes touching her and the clamp of his fingers around hers was starting to burn with electrical jolts. If Gracia didn't return soon, she might do something stupid like step right into his arms.

"I might not be Miss Rodeo, Matt, but I don't need a nag."

A low chuckle rolled past his lips and in spite of all of Juliet's self-warnings, she felt her heart lifting.

"Believe me, Juliet, there are no nags on the Sandbur."

"I'll take your word for it," she murmured.

His free hand was reaching toward her cheek when the sound of Gracia's returning footsteps sounded near the doorway.

Clearing his throat, he moved away from her and over to open the door.

"Here it is, Juliet," Gracia announced as she rushed into the small atrium carrying a pecan-colored cowboy hat with a rolled brim. "It's old, so don't worry about getting it dirty or anything."

Juliet took the hat and self-consciously plopped the headpiece over her blond hair. "Hope I don't scare the horses," she said teasingly.

Gracia laughed. "You look beautiful, Juliet. Just like a real cowgirl."

His expression guarded, Matt opened the

door and gestured for the two of them to proceed in front of him.

"Let's go," he said gruffly. "We need to get started if we're going to have lunch."

The morning had turned out to be warm with only a slight breeze to ruffle the new leaves blossoming on the trees. Birds were chattering from every direction and the sun was beating down with the promise of hotter days to come. Juliet had always enjoyed being outdoors and she had to admit that today was one of those halcyon days that happened only on rare occasions.

The horse Matt had chosen for her was a brown gelding with a blaze down his face and four white anklets. His name was Chigger and as Matt had promised he was far from a nag; he was beautiful and very obedient. She was having no problem controlling him or staying in the middle of the saddle as the three of them briskly clopped across the low rolling hills just west of the ranch yard.

"I haven't seen any cows," Juliet commented as she glanced around at the mesquite-dotted land. "Where are they?"

Matt was riding to the left of her and

Gracia to the right. Juliet glanced over at him when he spoke.

"You'll see some soon. The grass is better west of here. More rain has fallen there near the river. Most of the herds are on the northern range where they've been all winter. We expect to be moving them soon."

"Guess that takes a lot of work," Juliet replied.

"Every wrangler on the ranch is mounted and riding."

"I hear some ranches down here use helicopters and four-wheelers to gather their cattle," she commented. "What about the Sandbur?"

"Daddy would never do that," Gracia spoke up quickly. "He likes things done the traditional way—the cowboy way."

Matt smiled faintly at his daughter's reasoning. "Gracia is right, but not necessarily because I'm old-fashioned. Loud machines terrorize the cattle and send them running wildly to hide in hedge rose thickets and dense chaparral. They're so traumatized they usually have to be roped and dragged out. It makes for a lot of undue stress on the animal. And stress means loss of weight, which in turn means a loss of dollar. Men on horseback, gently prodding them along is the way it's been done for hundreds of years and it's still the best way."

"Makes sense to me," Juliet said, then smiled at Gracia. "Sounds like you know your father pretty well."

The girl shrugged both shoulders. "He likes to talk cattle, so I know a lot about how he does things here on the ranch."

Dear Lord, Juliet thought. Gracia had just turned thirteen; she needed conversations about school and clothes and boys and girlie things in general, not how to rope or brand a calf.

Ignoring Matt's presence for the moment, she asked, "What about when you want to talk about dresses or something like that?"

Gracia giggled loudly. "Daddy doesn't know *anything* about a dress. But I have Aunt Geraldine and Nicci to talk to. And sometimes, Daddy's sister, Lucita, comes to visit and I can talk to her. But that's not important anyway, 'cause I don't much like dresses—unless I'm going somewhere really fancy."

Surprised by the news that Matt had another sibling, Juliet looked over at him. His rugged profile was a smooth blank as he stared at the trail in front of them.

"You have a sister? I didn't know that. Was she at your cousin's wedding?"

Shaking his head, he said, "No. Unfortunately she couldn't make it. Her ten-year-old son was ill and wasn't able to make the trip up from Corpus Christi."

"Oh. That's too bad. Is that where they live?"

He turned his head slightly toward her then and Juliet could see faint lines of disappointment on his face.

"Yeah. Lucita teaches there in a public school."

"And Marti wants to come home to the Sandbur, too," Gracia interjected. "I wish he would. Then I'd at least have a young person to talk to."

Juliet didn't miss the grimace on Matt's face and she realized she was beginning to know the man. The first time she'd met him, she'd believed he was unfeeling. But now she was beginning to see that his family brought out all sorts of emotions in him.

"It would be nice if Marti and Lucita would come back home to live, Gracia. But she—" He paused and shook his head. "This is something we shouldn't be discussing in front of a guest, honey."

Throwing her shoulders back, Gracia frowned at him. "Juliet isn't a guest! She's a friend. And what would it hurt if she knew about Lucita? She won't tell anybody."

With her literally being in the middle, Juliet could feel the tense undercurrents between daughter and father as they stared back and forth. She tried to lighten the moment.

"Gracia, remember I'm a newspaper journalist," she said in a teasing tone. "My job is to spread the word."

"Yeah," Gracia replied. "But you wouldn't do something like that to our family."

Gilbert's menacing threat suddenly raced through Juliet's mind and she stared at her horse's ears rather than face Matt. "It's all right, Gracia. Your family's private lives are none of my business."

After that they rode along in silence for long moments. Juliet decided she needed to bring up another subject when Matt suddenly spoke.

"If Gracia wants you to know, then I'll tell you, Juliet. Lucita is divorced. She was— terribly wronged by her husband."

Gracia nudged Traveler closer to Juliet. "He was a cheater," she added with enthusiastic scorn. "He had a mistress."

Matt looked at his daughter with outrage. "Gracia! What are you doing using such a word? You don't even know what it means!" he scolded.

"Oh yes I do," Gracia informed him. "Aunt Geraldine explained it to me. And she says Marti's dad needs to be strung up by his—"

"That's enough!" Matt blasted at her. "I can see right now that I'm going to have a talk with Geraldine or you're going to have to stay away from the big house!"

Gracia eased back down in the saddle and clamped her lips shut.

Sighing, Matt looked at Juliet with dismay. "What is my aunt thinking, telling Gracia such stuff?"

Juliet tried to keep her smile to one of understanding rather than amusement. "Believe me, Matt, Geraldine is a mother and she knows what she's doing. Gracia is becoming a young woman. She has to hear things and learn things that you might not always approve of."

"Thank you, Juliet." Gracia spoke up, then to her father, she said, "Tell her the rest, Daddy. About Lucita."

With a roll of his eyes, he said, "The

bastar—the man stole all her money. When each of us siblings reached the age of twenty-five our parents gave us an allotment of money from their part of the ranch's profit. It amounted to many thousands of dollars and was meant to give us security in case we had problems. The jerk took it all and left."

A frown of disbelief marred Juliet's forehead as she looked at Matt. "How did he manage to get his hands on the money? Didn't she have it in a secure place?"

"Three banks. All in savings accounts. But her husband's name was also on all the accounts, so it was within the law for him to withdraw the money. It happened before Lucita had any idea he had plans to leave her."

Amazed, Juliet shook her head. "But surely if she took him to court—in the divorce—didn't the judge make it right?"

His jaw turned hard. "There was no divorce court or any kind of court. Vance couldn't be found. His whereabouts are still unknown and we figure he disappeared to Mexico."

Juliet asked, "Did the cops try to track him?"

"For a while. But the trail went cold and I suppose the law shoved the whole thing aside. Since there wasn't a murder or rape involved, they probably didn't consider the case a number one priority."

"But it was rape, Matt," Juliet argued. "He robbed your sister of her inheritance and much more. He should have to pay."

Matt looked at her. "Lucita didn't push for justice. She says her son is all that really matters to her. But now Lucita is having a tough time financially making ends meet. We want her to come home to live—we've tried to give her more money from the ranch, but she insists she doesn't deserve our help or the money."

"I'm so sorry, Matt. You must worry very much about her."

"I do. We all do. Every day that I go see Dad, he asks about his daughter. I know it would help him if he knew she was back on the Sandbur."

In spite of his earlier reluctance, Matt had let her into another part of his life, his family, and she could feel herself being drawn closer and closer to the man, to his problems, his sorrows, his joys. She realized with a start that she wanted to be a part of them and him. The notion was more than troubling and she tried her best to push it away.

"Well, there's one thing for sure," she said with a chuckle to lighten the moment. "No man will ever be guilty of marrying me for my money because I don't have any."

Across from her, Gracia smiled impishly. "You don't need any money, Juliet. Daddy has plenty."

"Gracia! So help me—"

Matt's yelled threat was lost on his laughing daughter as the girl spurred Traveler's sides and the horse shot forward in a gallop.

He stared after his daughter for a few seconds, then turned a hopeless look on Juliet.

"Sorry about that, Juliet. I don't know what's come over her."

Wanting to reassure him, Juliet reached over and touched his arm. "She was only teasing, Matt. I think she—understands that you don't want a wife."

"Yeah. Only teasing," he said grimly, then kicked his horse into a lope.

Juliet watched him chase after his daughter and wondered why neither of them was laughing.

Chapter Seven

Juliet urged Chigger into a short lope and found Matt and Gracia waiting for her over the next hill. Once she reached them, they continued west for another half hour or more through an area where the land was dotted thick with mesquite and shaded here and there with large live oaks. The grass grew taller and herds of Brahman could be seen grazing around huge clumps of prickly pear and wesatch.

Gracia had been quieter on this leg of the journey, but from Juliet's observations, she didn't appear to be sad or pouting. Apparently Matt hadn't given his daughter much of a scolding and Juliet was relieved. In fact, the girl seemed bubbly and Juliet figured just having her father out with her like this was enough to make her happy.

A half hour later, they reached the San Antonio. The sandy banks were steep, the water below deep and clipping along with a steady current. Since Gracia wanted to wade, Matt decided the three of them would have to ride north to a spot where sand deposits kept the water at a shallower depth.

It took another fifteen minutes before they arrived at a deep bend in the river where a sandbar narrowed the waterway. The bank was shaded with tall willows, wispy salt cedar and thorny mesquite. They chose a spot beneath one of the willows to spread their lunch and Matt tied their mounts nearby.

From their saddlebags, Juliet and Gracia pulled out the lunch fixings and a thin tablecloth to stretch across the sparse clumps of grass. While they worked to ready the meal, the teenager chattered nonstop and from where Matt stood a few steps away, he didn't miss the happiness on his daughter's face. When she was around Juliet, she was like a different girl. But then he had to admit that being around the woman made him a different man.

Seeing her again this morning had been like a rock lifting from his heart. He wanted to hum. He wanted to lift his face toward the blue sky and smile. It was a crazy reaction, he realized. But the feelings she induced in him were too pleasant to want to squash.

For their lunch, Juan had made huge sandwiches of smoked pork jammed between slices of homemade German bread. Along with the sandwiches, there were potato chips, baked beans and all sorts of condiments. To follow up with dessert, the old man had packed individual containers of dewberry cobbler. The crust was dusted with coarse ground sugar and though Juliet was certain she couldn't hold another bite, she couldn't resist the sweet concoction.

"Mmm. This is absolutely delicious," she mouthed between bites of the cobbler. "Do you have a cook that made this at your house or does the woman up at the Saddler house cook for you, too?"

"Cook strictly works for Aunt Geraldine, although lots of times she makes enough things to spread around the ranch," Matt explained. "We have a personal cook at our house, too. His name is Juan."

"And Juan knows how to make everything good," Gracia added. "But he always says he's not a cook, he's just a cowboy."

"Well, when we get back to the ranch, I'll make a point of telling him how delicious everything was," Juliet remarked, then glanced at Matt, who was lounging on the ground a short space away from her. "Did the man work as a cowboy? Or has he always been your cook?"

Matt shook his head. "No, Juan has been a cowboy all his life. But he hurt his hip last year and had to have the joint replaced. Thankfully, when I offered him the cooking job, he honestly did know how to throw a meal together."

Juliet laughed with disbelief. "You mean you hired him as cook and didn't know whether he could actually do the job?"

He shrugged. "I thought it would be easier on him."

So the man had more of a heart than she'd expected. The idea tugged on her like an invisible string, pulling her closer and closer to him.

Glancing over at him, she caught his gaze with hers. "That was very generous of you."

A semblance of a smile curved his lips, but he didn't say anything.

At the opposite end of the blanket, Gracia tossed her father a proud smile. "Daddy likes to help people. He treats everybody on the ranch like family. Unless they don't follow his orders. Then he yells."

Juliet laughed and Matt's faint smile deepened for a brief moment. The relaxed change in his expression caused Juliet's gaze to linger and the sight of him reclined upon the grassy ground, his muscled torso propped upon one elbow was sexy enough to send a ribbon of heat curling through her stomach.

Clearing her throat, she swallowed the last of the cobbler and placed the container out of the way. "Speaking of helping people," she commented, "your cousin Nicci has really helped me."

His brows peaked with curiosity. "Nicci? You know her?"

"I met her at Gracia's birthday party and I've talked to her since—about a friend of mine who works as a waitress at the Cattle Call. She's a single mother and can't afford medical care for her little girl. Nicci has agreed to be their doctor for only what my friend can afford."

"Are they poor?" Gracia asked with the frankness of a young person.

"Gracia! That's not a nice question," Matt corrected the teenager.

"Being poor isn't a nice situation, either," Juliet told him. "But I have a feeling that Angie won't always be down like this. She's going to college at night and working hard to do better."

"Well, Nicci's heart is as big as this ranch," Matt said. "If the clinic where she worked would allow it, she'd work for nothing. In fact, several times in the past she's traveled to third world countries and doctored needy people. I can tell you that she'll take good care of your friend and her child and they won't have to worry about paying for medicine. She has a way of doling out samples to the neediest."

Juliet knew he was speaking the truth of his cousin and from what she could gather, when it came to people needing help, Matt was just as generous. Yet Gilbert wanted her to do a malicious story about lust and greed regarding these people. The man was sadistic and if Matt knew what the newspaper editor had in mind, he'd probably want to choke the man, then turn on Juliet. But she wasn't going to tell him about Gilbert's plans. At least, not until she could decide how to best handle the situation.

After rubbing her palms uneasily against her thighs, Juliet reached for a stack of dirty napkins while trying to push the problem with Gilbert out of her mind. "Well, I don't know how I'll ever be able to show your cousin my gratitude. I realize she's probably bombarded with sad luck stories all the time. I'm just grateful she listened to mine."

At the opposite end of the makeshift table, Gracia popped the last of her sandwich into her mouth and jumped to her feet.

"I'm finished eating so I'm going wading. Want to come with me, Juliet?"

Juliet glanced up at the girl. "You go on. I'll be along in a few minutes after I put away the lunch things."

Gracia frowned with uncertainty. "Are you sure? I can help you."

Waving her on, Juliet said, "No. There are

only a few things. I'm going to sip a bit of your father's coffee, then I'll come down to the water."

The girl glanced from Juliet to her father and back again as though she liked the image of the two of them sitting fairly close together.

"Okay," she said breezily. "I'll be down below."

"Don't wander into the deep water," Matt spoke up. "And watch for rattlers."

"I will, Daddy. You just have a nice conversation with Juliet."

Before the teenager turned to climb down the riverbank, Juliet was certain she'd seen a calculating glint in her brown eyes. But that wasn't surprising. The very first time she'd seen Gracia sitting out on the lawn at the big ranch house, she'd expressed her wishes for a mother. Juliet supposed she should point out to the teenager that she was wasting her time in trying to be a matchmaker for her father. But the girl was too happy for Juliet to spoil her day in such a way.

Once Gracia was out of sight, Matt reached for the thermos of coffee sitting near him and passed it over to Juliet.

After thanking him, she poured a small

amount into a foam cup and sipped the rich liquid. "Want some?" she asked.

He shook his head and she smiled at him.

"So how are you enjoying this picnic? Bet you're lying there wishing you were back at the ranch helping your brother in the horse pen."

"Actually, I wasn't thinking anything of the sort. The day is beautiful. And it's not often that I get to see parts of the ranch in such a leisurely way." He glanced around him, then back to her. "I was just thinking that this was how my grandparents and great-grandparents must have seen this land when they first arrived here in south Texas. Just raw and wild and nothing on it, but mesquite and cactus, snakes and coyotes. If I'd lived back then I doubt I'd have had the fortitude or vision that they had to build the Sandbur."

Absently, she twisted the cup in her hand as her gaze searched his face. He'd taken his hat off before they'd started to eat and now the gentle breeze that fluttered the leaves above them teased his crow-black hair and splayed thick strands of it against his forehead.

The fringe of shiny locks softened his features and mentally lured Juliet toward him. With her eyes fixed on his lips, she said, "It must be nice to have such heritage. I only knew about my grandparents on my mother's side. The rest of my family—I don't have any idea about them. My father couldn't have cared less about his folks or his past and my mother was adopted. I guess some families are just bound together from the start and some aren't."

He pushed himself up to a sitting position and Juliet's insides quivered as his face ended up only inches away from hers.

"Even bound families have their problems, Juliet. The Sanchezes and the Saddlers have both had their share of problems and worries and heartaches."

She thought of Matt's wife and father, his sister's broken heart and sighed. "Yes, I suppose so."

Suddenly his green eyes softened and he reached up and cupped his hand alongside her face. "Do you know how it made me feel to see you this morning?"

Her heart went still, then leaped into a gallop. "No," she whispered.

His fingers moved ever so slightly against her cheek. "It made me happy, Juliet. Very happy."

Doubt pulled her brows together. "That doesn't sound like the Matt Sanchez I know."

"It isn't like him," he said slowly. "You do things to me, woman. Things I don't understand."

With every word he spoke, his face grew nearer until his lips were only a scant fraction away from hers. Juliet was frozen with anticipation, afraid to breathe or move or speak in fear that she would break the electric connection between them.

"I told myself I didn't want to invite you here today," he murmured. "I told myself I was only doing it for Gracia. But the moment I saw you I knew I'd been lying to myself. I wanted to see you again because I can't forget how you felt against me. I can't forget how much—I want you."

The last words were whispered against her lips and his warm breath was like a ray of sun coaxing the petals of a flower to unfurl. Her lips parted; her eyes closed and then she felt his kiss sweetly searching, tasting and urging her closer.

Her hands closed over the tops of his shoulders and the warmth of his flesh prompted her fingers to flex against his hard muscles.

For days she'd thought of nothing but this and struggled to deal with the fact that she would never experience being in his arms again. But now here she was and erotic sensations were bombarding her from all directions.

Her mouth opened and the tip of his tongue teased her teeth and her bottom lip, before he finally pulled back and rested his forehead against hers.

"If Gracia wasn't with us you'd be on this blanket and I'd be making love to you."

His frank words shocked her and her breath drew in sharply as she eased slightly back from him to search his face. "Matt— you—you said you didn't want anything like this between us. What—"

His hands reached up and framed the confusion on her face. "I know I've said lots of things to you, Juliet. And at the time I thought I meant them. But since then I've had second thoughts about you and me. About us. Maybe the two of us spending time together wouldn't really be all that dangerous."

Dangerous. The word seemed to fit the explosive nature of their relationship. Yet she wanted to believe as he did that the two of them could be together without either of them getting hurt.

She drew in a bracing breath while realizing her heart was hammering like a runaway engine. "Is that what you want, Matt? For us to spend time together?"

A crooked grin twisted his lips as he drew her face back to his. "What does this feel like?"

He began kissing her again, deeper this time and Juliet was about to curl her arms around his neck when Gracia's voice floated up to them.

"Juliet!" she yelled. "C'mon! The water is warm! It feels wonderful!"

Matt broke the kiss just as Juliet was about to jerk back from him. She looked at him in dazed wonder and a wry smile spread across his face.

"My child has great timing. You'd better go or she'll be up here trying to drag you down."

"Yes. I'd better go," she murmured and quickly rose to her feet. "What are you going to do?"

His eyes lazily swept up and down the length of her. "Don't worry about me. I have plenty to sit here and think about."

* * *

Three days later, Juliet was sitting at her desk, attempting to work while half her thoughts were on Matt, where they'd been ever since the day of the picnic. His change in attitude toward her had left her in a dazed sort of trance and she continued to wonder what had happened with the man. But did his motives even matter? In the end, all that should matter to her was that he finally seemed to trust her and he actually wanted to be with her. For a man like him that was like changing the moon into the sun, and she shouldn't be looking into the miracle that deeply. Some things just couldn't be explained.

A knock sounded on the open door to her office and Juliet glanced up to see Gilbert's wiry little self stepping toward her desk. The sight of the man sent her spirits plummeting.

"Madsen, I was just going over those photos you shot at the courthouse square. They're good, but I want another one with the workers on the scaffold, not standing down below it. They look lazy and the contractor isn't going to like seeing it in the newspaper and neither are the taxpayers."

If Juliet remembered correctly, the time

she'd shot the photos of the restorative work being done on the courthouse, the men had been on the ground digging some sort of footing, not standing around. But she wasn't going to argue with Gilbert. It would be easy enough to walk the two blocks to the courthouse and snap more pictures.

"No problem. I'll do it this afternoon," she assured him.

Nodding curtly, he glanced pointedly at her desk. "I've been expecting an update from you on the Ketchum story. How far have you gotten with it?"

No further than she had two weeks ago, Juliet wanted to tell him. Instead, she tried to think of a good stall. "Uh—I've been meaning to stop by your office and let you know I'm still doing research."

The constant frown on Gilbert's face turned into an all-out scowl. "Research! Madsen, I talked to you about this project two weeks ago. There couldn't be that much research!"

Laying down her pen, Juliet folded her hands atop her desk and gave him her full attention. "I hadn't expected there to be," she said. "But once I got to digging through the archives, I discovered there've been numerous articles done on the couple and the ranch. I need to assimilate all of them before I can do the piece any justice."

Moving to the corner of her desk, he jabbed his forefinger on a bare spot of the wood. "You've had time, Madsen. I want to see the piece finished by next week."

Images of Matt and Gracia floated through Juliet's mind and her stomach felt as though poisonous snakes were swimming in the pit of it and one wrong move could cause her to be fatally bitten.

"I can't do that," she said carefully. "I need more time."

Raking a hand over his balding head, he lowered a glare at her. "I'm getting the feeling that you're stalling, Madsen. Am I wrong?"

The meek approach had never been Juliet's style and she wasn't about to cower to Gilbert, even if he was her boss. She had personal principles that no one could make her toss aside.

"I'm just trying to get the full picture here, sir. I don't want my name attached to a piece that isn't fair and factual."

He snorted. "This isn't the *New York Times*

or even the *Houston Chronicle,* Madsen," he said sarcastically. "So what if you dramatize a little? No one around here is going to question or investigate us."

Her jaw dropped as she stared at him in disbelief. "Your father was known for running an ethical newspaper, Mr. Gilbert. I was under the impression that the *Fannin Review* was still an honored establishment in this town. Do you want that to change?"

Another snort erupted from the editor. "Honor. Principles. Since when did those two things sell newspapers? And what good will ethics do us, if we can't afford to keep the doors open on this place?"

Juliet was quite sure the newspaper was doing fine as far as financial security, which made Gilbert's attitude even worse.

"I don't know about you, Mr. Gilbert, but I'd never be willing to compromise my ethics for bigger sales. I have a higher value of myself than that."

The image of his scowling face reminded Juliet of a skinny bulldog, all wrinkles and teeth, but not enough inner strength to win the fight. At least, not with her, she thought grimly.

"That wouldn't be so easy for you to say

if you were sitting behind my desk, young lady." Then with a dismissive swat of his arm, he added, "Just give me something on the Ketchums, Madsen. And make it good."

Something good. The two words caused Juliet's mind to suddenly spin with an idea that should have already come to her before now. She could definitely handle a story with a positive element behind it. But would Gilbert? It was a chance she had to take.

Nodding with total concession, she said, "All right, Mr. Gilbert, I'll do my best to have the piece written by the end of next week. And I promise to make it something readers will enjoy."

Thankfully, the man looked somewhat mollified at her announcement and started toward the door. "This is it, Madsen. I expect it to be on my desk by the end of next week or there's going to be serious issues as to whether you keep this job."

Juliet bit down on her tongue to keep from flinging several curse words at the man. But as he exited the room, she silently flung her opinion of him at his back.

She was rubbing her fingertips against her

forehead and still trying to compose her anger when the phone on her desk rang.

Relieved at the interruption, she reached for the receiver.

"Madsen here."

"Juliet?"

The sound of Matt's voice brought her to instant attention and she bolted straight up in the desk chair. Thank goodness Gilbert had just left the room, otherwise the conversation could have been worse than awkward.

"Yes. Yes, it's me."

"You sound surprised to hear from me," he said with a bit of humor.

"I am. A little." The other evening, when she'd finally left the Sandbur after the picnic, the two of them had parted warmly. In fact, once Gracia had disappeared into the house, her and Matt's goodbye had been a heated kiss exchanged at the door of her car. Even so, she hadn't expected to hear from him this soon.

"Well, I don't mean to interrupt your work. I just called to ask you to dinner tonight. Are you free?"

Dinner with Matt? Juliet was well aware that the picnic invitation had initially been for Gracia's sake. But this was something different, something very personal, and the whole idea made her tremble. If she wanted to be a practical, safe woman, she wouldn't think twice. She'd gently decline with some sort of excuse. But wise or not, that wasn't what she wanted to do. Spending time with the man had turned into a craving.

"Juliet? Are you still with me?"

His voice jolted her out of her whirling thoughts and she stammered, "Er—yes—I'm here. I was just trying to remember if I had any obligations after work this evening. I don't think I do."

"Does that mean yes?"

Closing her eyes, she pushed her long hair off her forehead and drew in a bracing breath before she made the leap. "Yes. It means yes."

She heard a faint sigh on his end of the line and wondered wildly if he'd actually expected her to say no. Didn't the man know she was falling for him in the worst kind of way?

"Good. I'll pick you up about seven. Give me your address."

Her eyes popped open. "You mean we're not eating at the ranch?"

He chuckled. "No. But if you want to, I can

arrange it. I just thought you'd like to eat something other than ranch grub tonight."

And maybe he wanted the two of them to be alone, without Gracia or Cordero, or anyone else on the ranch around to interrupt them. The idea sent tingles of anticipation down Juliet's spine and she realized she was moving toward dangerous water, but it was too late to do anything about saving herself. She was too weak to fight the undertow.

"All right. I'll be ready," she said, then gave him the directions to get to her house.

After they'd exchanged goodbyes and she'd hung up the phone, Juliet fell weakly back in her chair and exhaled a heavy breath.

For long moments she stared unseeingly at the work on her desk, until her gaze finally settled on her empty ring finger. Once a diamond had sparkled there, given to her by a man who had showered her with attention and so-called love. She'd believed she and Michael had a future. She'd planned on it, worked toward it. But then everything had come tumbling down like a mud hut in a rainstorm and her loss had left her feeling just like that—homeless.

Since then, when it came to men, she'd

sworn to live a more careful life. She'd promised herself to never fall in love with a man who only wanted to use her. Is that what she was doing now, she asked herself, falling in love with Matt, a man who'd already told her he didn't want a woman in his future?

She couldn't answer that now. Not when all she could think about was being back in Matt Sanchez's arms.

Chapter Eight

Juliet was late getting home from work and ended up having only a half hour to shower and change into something suitable to wear. But since she had no idea where Matt was taking her to eat, she had to simply guess and try to choose something that would fit in at either a fast-food joint or a fine restaurant.

She ended up pulling on a cotton floral dress with a background of red roses. It had a cinched waist with a matching belt and a flared skirt that ended just above her knees. She added high-heeled sandals, golden hoops to her ears and a tiny cross of pearls around her neck.

Matt's knock came just as she was putting a last swipe of color to her lips. Quickly, she dropped the tube of coral lipstick into her handbag and, taking it with her, hurried to the front room to answer the door.

Juliet's residence was a surprise to Matt. He'd expected her to be living in an apartment where a renter didn't have to worry about maintenance to the structure or the lawn. He would have never pictured her living in a neat little clapboard house with flowers growing at the edge of the porch and a live oak shading the front yard. The homey image didn't match her Dallas background, but maybe she'd changed since moving from the big city. Matt wanted to think so. He wanted to believe she wasn't a fish out of water here, a fish that would eventually want to head back to the big, wide ocean.

His thoughts were interrupted when the door in front of him swung open and Juliet was silhouetted in the light coming from somewhere behind her.

The lines of her curvy body encased in a feminine dress was a sight for his hungry eyes and for a moment all he could do was stare and wonder why it had taken him so long to give in to his desire. Why had he fought this attraction so hard, when there were men who'd give their eye teeth and more for a woman like Juliet? It wasn't as if she could kill him. Maim his heart maybe. But that was a chance he had to take.

"Hello, Matt. I'm almost ready. Want to come in a minute while I finish?"

He stepped through the door and past her luscious body. Along the way her sweet perfume trickled to his nose and tempted him to simply turn and reach for her. But Matt was smart enough to know that once he touched her, he might not be able to stop. So he moved to the middle of the room and looked around him with interest.

"This is nice, Juliet. I would have never expected your home to look like this," he admitted, as he glanced around at the wooden rocking chair, the chintz furniture and a vase filled with Texas bluebonnets sitting on a drop leaf table. A fat black cat was curled up in the seat of the rocker and the animal looked up at him with lazy curiosity.

Smiling, she asked, "Really? What did you expect? Lots of frilly, girlie things?"

Shaking his head, he walked over to an end table where a photo stood of Juliet and an older woman standing in a pose together. He picked it up and studied their images.

"No. I had something more modern in mind. Like empty spaces, chrome fixtures and black-and-white walls—you know the type."

Her smile deepened. "I'm not that sterile, Mr. Sanchez. I'm cozy. I like people and things around me." She gestured toward the photo he was holding. "That's my mother with me. Before she became ill."

"She's beautiful. Like you."

He felt her edging up behind his shoulder and without turning to look, he could envision her body in that sexy dress, the way the fabric framed her bosom and exposed the satiny skin of her chest. The image sent subtle fingers of heat spreading through his body and he swallowed in an effort to ignore his growing desire.

"She was beautiful," she said softly. "Inside and out. There's never a day that goes by that I don't think of her and miss her."

Placing the photo back on the table, he turned to her, his expression wry. "It's too bad that both of our mothers are gone. I think you would have liked mine. She was a strong, opinionated woman—like someone else I know," he added with an impish grin.

Laughing softly at his insinuation, she opened her handbag and began to check the contents. "Then I know I would have liked her. And it would have been interesting to hear what she had to say about raising two sons like you and Cordero."

His smile changed to one of fond remembrance. "Gracia sáys the same thing. She was only around seven when her grandmother died so she didn't get to have any sort of adult conversations with her. But thankfully she does have memories and that's more than some children ever have. Like you, I suppose," he added soberly.

Nodding with a sad sort of acceptance, she snapped the bag shut, then turned toward an arched doorway. "I'll go lock the back door and we can be on our way. Or would you like something to drink before we head out?"

He'd like to forget the drink, the food and everything else, Matt thought helplessly. He felt like a rutting buck that had just woken up and realized he was about to miss the whole mating season.

"No thanks. We'll get drinks when we get there."

Matt drove her to an old historic house on the outskirts of town that had been turned into a restaurant that served both Mexican and traditional food. They both settled for Mexican and ordered cabeza, a spicy beef that they wrapped in flour tortillas and ate with refried beans and Spanish rice. The two of them washed it all down with salty margaritas and by the time the meal was finished, Juliet was stuffed and pleasantly relaxed.

She almost didn't notice when Matt pulled out of the driveway and turned the truck onto the highway headed west rather than back to town.

"What are you doing? My house is back that way," she said, gesturing behind them.

By now it was totally dark, yet she could see his profile in the illumination from the dashboard. The sensual grin on his face set her heart thumping.

"My sense of direction isn't confused. I thought we'd drive out to the ranch and have dessert. Cook sent over some of her famous pecan cake. I think you'll find it worth the drive."

The drive to the ranch wasn't just a short hop. It took almost thirty minutes to get to there from Goliad. But she wasn't going to point that out to the man—he'd lived here all his life. Apparently he had the time to waste and the cost of burning extra gasoline for the round trip would seem like pennies to a person with his financial means.

"Sure," she replied. "It'll give me an opportunity to say hello to Gracia."

As the truck began to pick up speed, he glanced her way. "Gracia won't be there. She's—uh—spending the night with her aunt Geraldine."

"Oh. Did she do this because you were going to be out of the house tonight?"

He turned his attention back on the highway. "No. It wasn't an issue of her being alone. Even though Cordero is off on a horse-buying trip, Juan is there." He cast her a sly smile. "If you're thinking I sent her off so that we could be alone, you're wrong. It was Gracia's idea to go up to the Saddler house. And it's not unusual. She likes to stay with her aunt and cousin from time to time. Sorta gives her a girls' night out."

He made it sound so casual and unplanned,

yet Juliet couldn't help wonder if this was more of Gracia's subtle matchmaking.

"What did she think about you taking me to dinner tonight?"

"What do you think? She thought it was grand. She was thrilled." His expression wry, he glanced at her. "I guess you've realized that she has this image of you becoming her mother."

Surprised that he'd already seen through Gracia's maneuvering, she squared around slightly in the seat and looked at him. "I didn't know you'd realized that."

He shrugged. "Sometimes I can be slow to understand my daughter. But on this count she's been pretty transparent."

Sighing, Juliet looked out at the darkened night and wondered what it would be like to be sitting here as his wife. What would her life be like sharing his home, his bed and life?

From the time she'd grown old enough to have a woman's thoughts and feelings, she'd longed for a home and family and all the deep roots that went with it. But the more she'd searched for that love and happiness, the more she'd seemed to get hurt. She didn't want to think that Matt was only going to be another name on her list of heartaches.

"I hope you haven't made a big deal of it with her," Juliet said quietly. "She's young— she doesn't understand that you have all sorts of reasons you don't want a wife."

He stared stoically ahead. "Yeah. All sorts of reasons," he murmured.

Juliet waited in hopes that he would say more on the subject. But he didn't and after a few moments passed he changed the subject completely and they finished the trip with small talk about her job at the newspaper.

When they arrived at the Sanchez house the only lights that appeared to be burning were on the front porch and the foot lamps lining the sidewalk. The night was warm and insects were singing a symphony as Matt took her by the arm and escorted her along the lighted path until they reached the front door.

It wasn't surprising to see him open the entrance without a key. The Sandbur was like a small village unto itself with its own special brand of security, mostly in the form of cur dogs that freely roamed the property.

He preceded her into the house and left her in the foyer until he'd turned on a lamp in the great room. Once she'd stepped into the larger area, he motioned for her to take a seat on the couch or in one of the stuffed armchairs flanking a huge stone fireplace.

"Have a seat and I'll go to the kitchen for the cake," he told her.

"I don't need to sit," she told him. "I'll come along and help you."

"Suit yourself," he said and gestured for her to follow him out of the room.

They traveled through a short hallway, then turned right into a spacious kitchen. A small lamp atop the fridge shed enough illumination for them to see without filling the room with glaring light. Juliet followed him over to a row of cabinets.

"Juan usually leaves the coffeemaker ready to go. All I have to do is flip the switch," he told her and reached over to the nearby machine to do just that.

"How nice," Juliet remarked. "I can't imagine having someone do all those things for me. I'd probably get to feeling spoiled."

He shot her a wry grin. "Don't get to thinking I have it easy. I get up at four and my day doesn't end until dusk."

Moving to another section of pine cabinets,

he pulled down two small plates and two matching cups, then took silverware from a drawer beneath. All the while Juliet watched the way his back muscles rippled beneath the thin fabric of his shirt, the way his jeans hugged his lean waist and hips. He was made like a man who spent endless hours in the gym, yet she was certain he'd never seen the inside of such a place much less exercised just for the sake of it. No, that lean, hard body of his came as a result of long tiring hours in the saddle.

Deciding she needed to get her mind elsewhere, Juliet looked around her. "Is there anything I can do? If you'll show me where the cake is, I can do the slicing."

He pointed to a plastic container on a nearby dining table. "Right there. I'll get one of those things to cut it with."

The thing he meant turned out to be a pie server. Juliet took the tool and sliced him a hefty piece of the stacked cake and a much thinner one for herself.

After the coffee was ready, Matt asked, "Do you want to eat in here or in the great room?"

She glanced around the cozy kitchen with its red checked curtains, varnished pine cabinets and plenty of potted succulents. "This is nice. Besides, we won't have to worry about crumbs in here."

He cast her a droll look as he pulled out a chair for her. "We wouldn't have to worry about the crumbs in there, either. We have three maids that keep both places running clean and smoothly. They need something to do."

Just one more giant difference in their lifestyles, Juliet thought, as she took a bite of Cook's pecan cake.

"Mmm. This is delicious," she said. "You're right, it was worth the trip out here."

Lines of amusement creased Matt's face as he watched her dig into the cake. "What about the company?" he asked suggestively.

She looked up and Matt's gaze zeroed in on a morsel of icing stuck to her lips. He was thinking about leaning across the corner of the table and kissing it off when the tip of her tongue appeared and did the job for him.

"I'm enjoying the company very much."

His hand slid across the tabletop until his fingers were touching her bare forearm. "You must be a forgiving person," he said wryly. "Otherwise you wouldn't be sitting here."

Her brows peaked with curiosity. "What does that mean?"

His fingers slid upward to her elbow, then back down to her wrist. Her skin was like touching warm cream and it wasn't difficult to imagine how it would feel beneath his lips.

"I behaved in a pretty obnoxious way when we first met."

She laughed. "That's putting it gently. But to be fair, you didn't know me. Or trust me."

He shrugged one shoulder. "Our family can't be as trusting as most. When you have money and—a history—people are out to take advantage. And since Dad is incapacitated now, I feel responsible for everyone here on the Sandbur."

Juliet reached for her coffee. "You don't have to explain."

His lips slanted with regret. "Don't I? When I think of some of the things I've said to you—well, I don't feel too proud of myself. But I want you to know that I...trust you now. I know you wouldn't deliberately do anything to hurt me or my family."

Gilbert's threat pushed through Juliet's head like a steamroller, but she couldn't bring herself to tell Matt about the editor's persistent idea to write a seedy story about the Ketchum family. In a few days, when she felt their relationship was on firmer ground, she'd approach him on the subject. But not tonight. Tonight was too special and she wasn't about to spoil it.

"You have my promise on that," she said softly, then feeling a bit awkward, she made a general gesture to the room. "Ever since I visited the other day, I've been curious about this house. I was surprised to see this plantation-style structure. Especially when the other house is hacienda style. Who built this one?"

Settling back in his chair, he sipped his coffee, then said, "My parents. They took a trip to Houston once and my mother saw a house like this. She told Dad she wanted one just like it and he came home and hired a contractor. Before that, they lived with Geraldine and her husband, Paul, in the big house. But that was long before either sister had all of their children and there was plenty of room for both families."

"I see," Juliet said wistfully as she imagined the large family living together. "And how romantic of your father to build your mother her dream house. He must have adored her."

His expression reflective, Matt nodded. "He loved her madly. And I thought—we all thought—that when Mother died our father would fall to pieces. Instead, he surprised us by being very strong. He told us that was the way Elizabeth wanted him to be and I guess even after she was gone, he couldn't let her down."

Complete devotion. She'd heard about real couples in love and together for all their lives, but she often doubted she would be that fortunate, to find a man who would stick by her side through good and bad. "What happened to Elizabeth?" she asked curiously.

His fingers moved to the top of her hand where they slid back and forth over her skin, as though touching her comforted him. Instinctively, Juliet turned her palm upward and clasped her fingers around his. Her action caused their eyes to meet and she felt a connection far deeper than any kiss they'd shared.

He said, "She had diabetes, which caused several other health complications. In the end, her heart failed. Since she was only fifty-six at the time, we all felt robbed and even angry, I guess, that we didn't have her for many years. But after a while the whole family came to realize we were just lucky to have had her for any amount of time."

Her eyes soft, she gently squeezed his hand. "You were lucky, Matt. When you were talking about your father's love for your mother I was thinking, wondering how my life would have been different if my parents' marriage had been that devoted and real. What I remember most is my mother shedding thousands of tears and my father constantly turning his back on her. I grew up hating him and vowing to never be in the position my mother was in."

Frowning, he asked, "Why didn't she get out of it?"

Juliet sighed. "In the end I suppose she was too weak and sick to make such a traumatic move for herself. But initially, when she was still young and healthy—well, I just don't know. Ultimately, I think she was too charmed by him to get out from under his spell."

His gaze caressed her face. "Is that really why you haven't married yet? Because of your father?"

Matt's questions surprised her, even bothered her, because it made her face parts of her life she wasn't all that proud of.

"Maybe. Deep down I guess it worries me that I'll fall for someone that isn't good for me and then wind up being as helpless and hurt as my mother." Sighing, she rose from the table and carried her empty plate and cup to the sink. "I almost married Michael, not knowing that he had other women on the side. When I found out about them and broke our engagement, he begged me to take him back and promised he would change. I was almost tempted to believe him. But I kept hearing my father make those same promises to my mother and that gave me enough strength to walk away and not look back."

Rising from his chair, he moved to her side. Juliet's heart fluttered as his hand curved against the side of her neck.

"I'm glad you didn't look back, Juliet."

His murmured words filled her eyes with surprise. "Does that mean you're glad I'm here instead—with you?"

His dark green eyes thoughtfully searched her face. "I've brought you here to my home. That should tell you how I feel."

Moving closer, she rested her palms against his chest. "You're a hard man to understand, Matt. Ever since I met you I've had the impression that you're still in love with your late wife. Am I right?"

Frowning, he said, "Why would you think that?"

Her gaze fell to the middle of his chest where her fingers were splayed against hard muscles. "You've said you weren't interested in ever getting married again. I just assumed that was because you still loved your wife."

He sighed. "If you're asking me if I'm still *in* love with my wife, then the answer is no. She's gone. And you can't be in love with a memory. At least, I can't. I remember her with love. But it was our marriage and her death that…changed me."

Glancing up at him, she gently searched his face. "Your marriage—it was good, wasn't it?"

His expression wry, he stepped away from her and began to move aimlessly around the room. Juliet's gaze followed him as she hoped and wondered if he finally felt close enough to open up to her.

"There were good times," he finally agreed. "And then there were other times that—well, Erica was from the East Coast. I met her in Fort Worth while I was there at a cattleman's convention. She was there with a group of other models in town to do a fashion show for a big charity event. We happened to be staying in the same hotel and our paths crossed in, of all places, the elevator. We had a whirlwind courtship and married a few months after we met. She knew nothing about ranching or living a rural life, but I will admit she worked hard to fit in."

"Then she must have loved you."

He paused at the table's edge to glance her way. "She did love me, in her own way. But I think it was more like she was in love with the image I represented. You know, the Wild West cowboy, the rancher, the macho Mexican who rode bucking horses and roped bulls. At the time I met her, I really didn't care why she was so attracted to me. She was beautiful and fascinating and I wanted to bring her here to the ranch and keep her all for myself—like putting a colorful, but fragile butterfly in a glass jar so I could always have it at hand."

Juliet wanted to walk over to him, to touch him in a reassuring way, but she didn't want to divert his thoughts. She wanted to hear about this beautiful Erica who had once shared his life and borne his child.

"You make it sound as though you shouldn't have married her," Juliet stated with a frown. "Is that how you feel?"

He shrugged as he turned his gaze to a darkened window across the room. "Sometimes. I don't know. I've always felt guilty about her death. I should have been watching her closer, making sure she wasn't doing something dangerous."

Juliet's frown deepened. "For heaven's sake, Matt, she wasn't a child that you had to keep constant watch over."

"No. But she was—well, she was constantly doing things behind my back. Not necessarily bad things, but doing them nonetheless. It caused problems between us, because I felt I couldn't trust her. Not when she refused to be completely open with me about everything. On the morning of the day she was killed, I found airline tickets to Greece that she'd purchased without ever mentioning anything to me. We quarreled about it and I told her she'd wasted the money because I wasn't going anywhere with her."

Her heart aching for him, Juliet moved across the room to where he stood. His face was full of defeat and she realized she desperately wanted to take it all away, to make him laugh and smile and love again. "Oh, Matt, maybe she was planning a surprise for just the two of you."

Shaking his head, he glanced down at her. "If it had been a one-time thing, I would have seen it that way, too. But things like that went on all the time with Erica and they were getting worse, not better. That morning when we argued about the tickets, I told her we were going to have to have a serious talk about our marriage and then I left the house. Lex and I had work to do over in a far range of the ranch. While we were gone, Erica went down to the stables and ordered one of the wranglers to saddle up a horse she'd never ridden before. It was spirited and I told her that I didn't want her on it."

"But she took advantage of you being gone and defied you." Juliet stated the obvious.

Nodding grimly, he said, "Lex and I were riding back to the ranch when we found her. And all I could do was ask myself over and over why she'd done it. To spite me, I'm sure. But I'm just as certain she didn't think the reckless little ride would take her life. She wasn't suicidal—just high-spirited."

Reaching up, Juliet touched his arm. "I'm so sorry, Matt."

His eyes were solemn as he lifted a finger to her cheek and traced a gentle circle upon her skin. "I've spent the past seven years trying to forget and telling myself I wouldn't ever trust another woman. But now you've come along and I realize I have to trust you." His head bent and his lips brushed her ears. "Because I want you, Juliet. Very much."

Her knees trembled and she clutched the front of his shirt at the same time his arms came around her.

She whispered, "Matt, I—I'd be lying if I said I didn't want you, too."

His hands cradled the back of her head and tilted her face up to his. "Juliet, my darling."

The sweet endearment hardly had time to register in her brain before his lips descended on hers in a kiss so hot and hungry that all Juliet could do was hang on to him and hope her legs wouldn't buckle.

His hands left her face and met at the small of her back where he tugged her forward and against his body. Like a cat arching toward a warm, loving hand, she leaned into him and deliberately settled her hips to his, her breasts to his chest.

The seductive move caused him to moan deep in his throat and the sound sent heat swirling through Juliet's body. Her heart hammered like a wild thing as she opened her mouth and invited his tongue inside.

Round and round, her senses whirled as his hands roamed her back and hips, his tongue thrust deep into the cavern of her mouth and stroked in an erotic rhythm all its own.

By the time he lifted his head, she was breathless, her body completely boneless and she gazed at him through a rising fog of desire.

His shadowed face was solemn and etched with need, his eyes were searching, questioning, even as they caressed. "I want to make love to you, Juliet."

He'd already told her that much with his kiss, she thought. But she supposed the words were giving her a chance to tell him no or to reach for a scrap of sanity that would convince her to walk away from him. But she could do neither. Not when her body was burning for him, her heart aching to be close to him.

"I want that, too," she whispered. "But your brother—"

"Won't be home tonight. Neither will Gracia." His hands slid quickly over her shoulders and down her arms. "I didn't purposely plan it that way, Juliet. But I'll be the first one to say I'm damn glad we're alone."

Her heart thundering in her ears, she didn't say a word. Instead, she simply placed her hand in his and let Matt lead her out of the kitchen.

Chapter Nine

At the far end of the great room was a staircase, which led to a group of bedrooms. The landing was lit with tiny night-lights and as Matt led her along, she got a vague sense of the splendor of the house. Glimpses of varnished cypress floors and crystal doorknobs were a reminder of just how much their lifestyles differed. Yet the warmth of Matt's hand around hers felt real and right.

Near the end of the landing, Matt pulled her through a partially opened door, then shut and locked it behind him. The realization of being secluded in a dark, private space with him was enough to heighten her senses even more, and by the time he led her to the bed, her skin was tingling, her heart beating so fast she was very nearly breathless.

"Is this your room?" she whispered.

"Yes."

He left her for a moment and then a tiny lamp in a far corner of the room suddenly shed an arc of dim light around them and across a king-size bed covered with a maroon comforter.

She didn't have time to see more as he returned to her side and drew her back into his arms. He kissed her lips, then moved on to plant rows of kisses down her throat and onto her shoulders. As he tasted and teased her heated skin, his hands began to work on the zipper at the back of her dress.

When it fell in a heap around her feet and his hands reached for the front snap of her bra, she moaned with desperation and began to fumble with the buttons on his shirt. After that, their movements became hurried and reckless. Clothes dropped to the floor and fell onto the bed, until both of them were undressed and their heated bodies tangled in a heap in the middle of the mattress.

Over and over Matt kissed her lips and face while her hands raced up and down his back, over his lean hips and broad shoulders. His bronze skin was smooth and hot and she touched her lips to every available spot she could reach.

"I've wanted you like this for so long," he murmured, once he lifted his head to look down at her. "And now—I can't get enough of you. I don't know if I'll ever get enough of you."

His words caused a flood of emotion to pool in her heart and Juliet looked up at him with misty eyes. She wanted him to say he loved her. She wanted to hear him promise the two of them would be together like this for the rest of their lives. Those earnest wishes were something she could admit to herself now. But not to him. Not yet. Tonight it had to be enough that he wanted her in his bed.

Her face full of yearning, she reached up and traced a finger along his hard cheekbone. "After you kissed me at the wedding, I spent more than a week telling myself I didn't like it. But I was lying to myself. Because I knew—I was sure that—"

His head dipped and his lips began a lazy foray upon one breast. "You were sure about what?" he urged in a whisper against her satiny skin.

Thrusting her fingers into his thick hair, she slid them against his scalp and guided his head so that his lips were at the center of her breast. As soon as his teeth closed gently around the already hardened nipple she groaned as pleasure shot through her like a sweet arrow.

"That you—would never take a second look at me," she said, her voice husky with need.

He chuckled and the sound vibrated through her body to warm her heart.

"You're the sexiest woman I've ever laid eyes on," he said as his lips explored the valley between her breasts. "Why wouldn't I take a second look?"

"Because you hated me—or should I say hated what you thought I stood for. But, Matt—"

Lifting his head, he placed a shushing finger over her lips. "I made assumptions that were wrong, Juliet. But none of that matters now. I've come to realize this is where you belong." Bending back to her, he rested his forehead against hers. "And I think you feel that way, too."

The gentleness of his words was unexpectedly tender and it swept her up on a golden cloud as she clasped his face between her hands and whispered, "Oh yes, Matt. This is where I belong."

Lifting her lips to his, she kissed him slowly, sweetly as she tried to express the fullness of her heart, the indescribable need she had for him. But after a moment a fire began to build between them and Matt took control with his tongue and his teeth as they nipped and searched and teased her mercilessly.

Juliet was breathless and on fire with longing when he finally eased his head back far enough to gaze down at her, and as he looked deep into her eyes, she thought how easy, how right it felt to be lying here with him.

"I hope you're protected with some sort of birth control because I don't have any condoms around here," he muttered wryly. "Maybe if I rummaged around in Cordero's room—"

He broke off as she began to shake her head. "That isn't necessary," she assured him. "I'm on birth control. No need to worry. But Matt—" Her brows puckered with confusion, she raised up on one elbow so that she was facing him. "Are you telling me that you don't keep condoms because—" Knowing she wasn't phrasing her question quite right, she stopped and started again, "When you said you didn't involve yourself with women, you meant that literally?"

With a self-mocking twist of his lips, he rose up on the side of the bed and gave her a sidelong glance. "That's exactly what I meant. Since Erica's death, I haven't been with a woman in any respect. I haven't wanted to be with one. Until you."

For a moment she was overcome by his confession as she tried to grasp what it all meant to him and to her. And then with a little cry, she scrambled to her knees and flung her arms around his neck.

"Oh, Matt," she whispered fervently as she smattered kisses across his face and down his neck. "Let me make love to you. Let me make this special—as special as I can for you."

With a hand against his chest, she nudged him back to the mattress and once he was lying flat, promptly draped herself over him. Instantly, his arms came around her waist to hold her tight, while he buried his face into the curve of her shoulder, where he mouthed against her, "You already have, my darling."

His words were like precious diamonds dropping into Juliet's heart, plugging the holes of lonely uncertainty that she'd carried for so long. Matt wanted her and no one else. The fact filled her with an incredible glow that filtered out through her lips as she kissed him, through her fingers as she stroked him.

Like dry kindling on a rain-starved desert, the contact of their bodies sparked into flames and driving need quickly took control of their movements.

When Matt finally rolled her onto her back and entered her with one hard thrust, Juliet's senses soared to a higher place where there were no sights or sounds, only golden clouds enveloping them with delicious heat.

For Matt, he couldn't touch her enough. His lips couldn't stop kissing hers or tasting her soft skin. His hands kneaded her breasts until other places called, like her hips and thighs and the concave beneath her belly button. And each place his fingers explored was followed by the hungry search of his lips, the seductive glide of his tongue. Until the burning need in his loins took complete control and the only thing he could focus on was driving himself deeper into her heated body.

His thrusts grew desperate and frenzied. Sweat rolled down his face and onto his chest. Beneath him, he could hear her soft cries of pleasure, feel each rise of her hips as they met his to give him more. And then more.

Matt tried to pause the need clawing at his body, to keep the incredible fire between them burning forever, but it was impossible to hold back the storm raging inside him. He'd drunk and drunk from her, filling his thirsty soul; now all he could do was pour everything, even his heart, back into her.

Long moments passed before Juliet realized she was back on earth, lying in the middle of Matt's bed. The heavy weight of his warm body anchored her to the mattress, making it impossible to move. But even without it, she couldn't have found the strength to lift her hand. She was drained. And yet she'd never felt happier or more complete in her life.

As her breathing slowed, so did Matt's, and eventually he rolled off her. Lying on his side, he reached to push the tangled blond hair from her face.

"I hope I didn't hurt you," he said.

She opened her eyes and with a drowsy smile summoned enough strength to roll toward him. "I've never felt so wonderful."

Her hand rested on his chest just as he was releasing a heavy breath and she realized he'd been anxious about her response. The notion made her marvel that he could doubt himself or her reaction. He'd filled her with so much joy she'd thought she might burst from it.

With a groan of relief, he pulled her toward him and she slipped her arm around his waist and cuddled the front of her body next to his.

"Neither have I," he said as he rested his cheek against hers and stroked the back of her head.

"Then you're not—sorry about this?"

With a comical frown wrinkling his face, he eased his head back to look at her. "Now why would I be sorry?"

As she gazed upon his dark features, she realized he'd become everything to her. All her hopes and dreams had somehow slowly wrapped around this man and it was impossible to separate them. And Juliet prayed she would never have to. Because she loved him.

There was no use trying to deny what was already in her heart.

"Oh, I don't know. Maybe because you waited so long and I—"

She broke off as doubts trickled through her mind like slow-moving molasses. Yet her expression must have conveyed some of her concerns, because he placed a comforting hand alongside her face.

"Juliet, my sweetheart, don't ruin the rest of our night with questions. Morning will be here soon enough and I want us to enjoy the time we have left."

Dipping his head back to hers, he began to nuzzle a row of kisses along her throat and across her chest. The enticement was enough to distract her and hardly a moment passed before desire, low in her belly, began to resurge with a vengeance.

Wrapping her arms around him, she said, "I want the same thing, too, Matt. Very much."

By noon the next day Juliet thought her head would be falling against her chest from the lack of sleep, but when she left the newspaper office to walk down to the Cattle Call, she felt like skipping and singing. There wasn't a tired bone in her body and the radiance must have shown on her face when Angie came to take her order.

"Wow! Did you get some sort of new makeup or something? You're positively glowing today," the waitress remarked as she pulled an order pad and pencil from her apron.

Propping her chin on a fist, Juliet gave the other woman a wide, dreamy smile. "No new makeup. I just feel good today."

After a furtive glance around the busy diner to make sure another customer wasn't waiting, Angie slid into the chair opposite Juliet. Leaning over the table, she said in a low voice, "All right, tell me what's happened and don't try to say it's nothing but a happy day. I've never seen you looking like this."

Juliet's smile turned a little wicked. "Sorry. I can't do that. It's too personal. Let's just say things are changing for the better."

Leaning back in her chair, Angie rolled her eyes. "Oh God, you must be talking about a man. Now I'm actually getting worried."

A frown replaced Juliet's grin as she placed her handbag under her chair. "Don't start getting all cynical on me, Angie. Women do need the male race once in a while. Even you."

The other woman's head wagged thoughtfully back and forth. "Maybe. But usually wherever a man walks, trouble walks right behind him and then a woman has two things to deal with."

Trying not to let Angie's dour attitude get to her, she pointed a finger at the waitress. "You need to get out more. And by the way, how's Melanie doing?"

At the mention of her daughter, the waitress's expression went soft. "Fit as ever," she said fondly. "And if I haven't thanked you before for giving us Doctor Saddler, then I'm thanking you again. I've never been one to ask for charity and I—"

"It isn't charity to ask for help once in a while," Juliet corrected her. "Especially when the asking is for a loved one rather than yourself."

Thoughtful now, Angie began to draw doodles on the edge of the small order sheet. "Yeah, I guess you're right. And Doctor Saddler is really, really nice. She didn't make me feel belittled in any way. I was surprised. I thought with her being from that family on the Sandbur that she'd have her nose in the air a bit. But maybe they're just regular folks like we are, Juliet. Isn't that a thought?"

No, Matt could never be a regular man, Juliet thought. Even if he didn't have a dime, he'd be special in her eyes. He'd driven her home this morning in the wee hours before the crew began to stir out in the ranch yard. And though the two of them had been alone in the house, she'd known he'd ended their time together because he'd wanted to protect her reputation and not have the wranglers seeing her leave the ranch at an indecent hour. In many ways he was a gentleman and that thought curved her lips with a faint smile. The first time she'd met him, she'd believed he was a heathen. How much her image of the man had changed since then, she mused.

"Well, the Saddlers and Sanchezes might be regular folks in lots of ways, but they'll never be like us, Angie."

Her expression a little weary, the waitress rose from the chair. "You're probably right about that. And I've got to get back to work. Better tell me what you want to eat. A salad?"

Juliet waved a dismissive hand at her. "No way. I want a big greasy cheeseburger with potato chips on the side."

Angie looked as though she'd been struck with a two-by-four. "Have you gone crazy?"

Chuckling, Juliet said, "No, I missed breakfast and I'm very hungry."

Shaking her head, Angie pointed an accusing finger at her. "There's something wrong with you and sooner or later you'll tell me about it."

The only thing wrong with Juliet was a desperate yearning to be with Matt again. But this morning when he'd dropped her off, he hadn't mentioned calling her or even when the two of them might get together again.

Still, she couldn't believe their time apart would last for long. Not if he'd felt anything close to what she'd experienced in his arms.

"Maybe in our golden years, Angie. When all we have are our memories."

Later that afternoon, Matt was in one of the barns gathering ear tags and vaccination equipment when Lex walked up behind him.

"There you are. I've been hunting everywhere for you," his blond cousin said. "What are you doing in here? I thought we were going to ride out to range five and look over that herd. Williamson, that buyer in Clovis has been ringing my phone off the hook. I've got to ship him something just to shut him up."

"I forgot," Matt said. "And I told the boys we were going to work the cattle here at the ranch yard before we moved them out to pasture. They've been penned for three days. They're losing weight and I want them on grass as soon as possible."

Shoving the supplies into a duffel bag, Matt turned to face the other man, then wished he hadn't when Lex started to whistle under his breath.

"Hellfire, you look like you've been run over by a steamroller."

"Thanks, cuz," Matt quipped with sarcasm. "You always were a real charmer."

Lex leaned in closer to inspect the lines around Matt's eyes. "What's the matter? Didn't you get any sleep? I thought—" His words suddenly broke off as something suddenly registered with him and he grinned with pure mischief. "Oh yeah, how could I forget. Gracia stayed at the house last night. She said you had a date with the newspaper-woman. How did that go? From the looks of you, not good."

Growling with frustration, Matt bent to zip

the duffel bag closed. "Even though it's none of your business, it went fine. Just fine."

Lex began to chuckle and Matt lifted his head to cast him a hard glare.

"Oh. I'm beginning to see the light. And thank God you have, too."

"Lex, I'm warning you to keep that big trap of yours shut or you're going to be eating dirt and plenty of it."

The other man was still chuckling when Matt's cell phone began to ring. He pulled the small instrument out of his pocket and answered, "Matt here."

"Matt, it's Geraldine. I'm sorry to disturb you and I won't keep you but a minute. I just wanted to give you an invitation to supper tonight. Nicci is actually going to come home early for one evening and we—the two of us—thought you might like to bring Juliet with you."

Matchmaking from his aunt? If it weren't for Lex being present, he could have laughed out loud. If only his family knew just how matched he'd already been with Juliet.

"Geraldine, Juliet and I already had supper together last night. Surely Gracia told you."

"She did. But what does two nights in a

row hurt? I'm sure the woman will have to eat somewhere and Cook is grilling rib eyes tonight."

He turned a droll look on Lex. "Is your son going to be there?" he asked his aunt.

The woman chuckled. "I don't know. You'll have to ask him."

"I won't bother," he muttered, then in a more serious tone, added, "Okay, count us in. That is, if Juliet can make it."

"I'm sure you can persuade her, honey. See you at seven," she said happily. "And don't worry about Gracia. She'll be staying over with me again tonight."

His family was obviously maneuvering him. But why should that bother him when being with Juliet was the only thing his mind wanted to contemplate. Talk about having it bad, he thought wryly. He was worse than a lovesick bull separated from his herd of heifers.

"All right, Geraldine," he said. "We'll be there."

He punched the off button and slipped the phone back into his shirt.

Lex studied him with a keen eye. "All kidding aside, Matt, I want you to be happy. I've wanted that for a long time. And I'm hoping this woman turns out to be everything you need."

Matt wiped a weary hand over his face. "I don't know, Lex. I wasn't looking for this to happen. But it has and now she's gotten a hold on me. If she isn't right for me—then I'm in for a hell of a time."

Seeing the anxious shadows in Matt's eyes, Lex reached over and gave his cousin's shoulder an encouraging squeeze. "Come on, cuz, let's get to work."

Later that evening, as the sun began to dip behind the mesquite-covered hills, Juliet found herself once again in Matt's truck and on her way to the Sandbur ranch. Only an hour earlier, she'd arrived home and walked into her kitchen to prepare herself a snack. When the telephone rang and it had been Matt inviting her to have dinner with him, she'd been taken by surprise. She'd been thinking, even hoping he'd be calling her soon, but she'd never expected to hear from him this quickly.

It had taken her only a few split seconds to assure him she'd be ready to go. The idea of hemming and hawing, as some women did just to keep a man wondering, had never entered Juliet's mind. After last night, it would have been stupid to try to hide her eagerness to be with him. The intimacy they'd shared was beyond petty dating games.

Glancing over at him, she said, "I have to admit that I was surprised to hear from you this evening."

A wry twist to his mouth, he said, "I wasn't going to call you. I figured you were tired. But I could tell Geraldine was eager for us to come."

Juliet was tired all right. At the most she'd gotten three hours of sleep and her body was sore in places she'd not even known existed. Yet none of that mattered. Just looking over at his rugged profile and tough, lean body was enough to fill her with excitement and longing. She knew the evening was going to be a long one until she could be alone with him again.

"I'm glad she wanted us to be there," Juliet told him. "Does she invite you over to her house very often?"

Matt shrugged. "Oh, three or four times a month probably. It gives Lex and I, and sometimes Cordero, a chance to talk about the business side of the ranch. And Geraldine enjoys having family around her for any reason. Nicci is so tied up at the clinic that she's rarely around and her younger daughter, Mercedes, is in the air force. So my aunt has to mostly settle with us hairy old guys for company."

Smiling wistfully, Juliet gazed out the passenger window. "I'm sure you men make her happy. Especially since she's a widow. If I might ask, what happened to her husband?"

"Paul?" A frown tugged his brows together as he stared ahead at the highway. "He was killed in a boating accident down on the gulf near Corpus. He'd gone out with some of his old cronies that he'd worked with at Coastal Oil. Somehow he went overboard without anyone seeing. By the time they turned the boat around to go after him, the waves had sucked him under."

Shocked by his brief account, she turned her head to look at him. "Did they ever find his body?"

His frown deepened as he tossed her another glance. "Yes. Why would you ask such a thing?"

Realizing she must have sounded like a lawyer, or even worse, a nosy journalist, she said, "I'm sorry if I sounded heartless, Matt. It's just—my mind is trained to assimilate facts and the story somehow sounds flimsy. But if the incident was ruled as an accident, then I guess there's no reason to consider it suspicious."

His expression turned to wry admiration as he focused his gaze back on the highway. "You're sharp, woman. Funny that you should be so quick to come to that notion. Geraldine has always thought there was more to Paul's death than what the police released in their report."

"Was an autopsy done?"

Matt nodded grimly. "The coroner said it looked as though Paul had suffered a heart attack and that's what had caused him to fall over the edge of the boat. But Paul had never had any sort of heart ailment. He went for regular tests and checkups with his doctor. He didn't smoke and exercised regularly. It didn't make sense. But then God has his own ideas about when a person's time is up."

Juliet's thoughts turned to Geraldine as she tried to imagine the unbearable loss she'd suffered. If Matt was suddenly taken from her, for any reason, how would she, could she go on? He'd already become too much a part of her to be able to survive without him.

Turning her mind away from the uneasy thought, she said, "You're right. But sometimes evil people intervene."

"Hmm. Well, Geraldine thinks it odd that two of Paul's old buddies later ended up making millions selling their shares of the oil company. There were rumors that insider trading had gone on, but that fact was never proved, so a case was never opened and Paul's was closed and marked accidental death."

She stared at him with something like horror. "Matt! A good investigator should have been brought in. Geraldine—"

"Was worried," he said with a shake of his head. "At that time she said Paul had been behaving oddly. Something had him greatly distracted. She'd started to think it might be another woman, but after his death, she feared it had something to do with the company. She believed Paul was a good, honest man, but when he refused to discuss anything with her, she couldn't help but wonder and worry. Then when he died so suspiciously, she decided it would be best not to drag up what might best be left buried with him."

Juliet nodded thoughtfully. "I can understand that. He was gone and loving memories were all she had left. She didn't want to lose them, too."

He looked at her with surprising tenderness. "You're thinking like a woman now, Juliet. Instead of a reporter."

Her heart swelled as she reached across the seat for his hand. He readily gave it to her and she squeezed his fingers.

"You might not believe it, Matt, but the woman in me wins out every time."

"I'll try to remember that, honey."

Chapter Ten

A few minutes later, they arrived at the Saddler house. To Juliet, the majestic home looked almost as it did the day she attended Raine Ketchum's wedding. Except the living room wasn't cleared of furniture for dancing and the hordes of laughing, partying people filling up every nook and cranny of every room were now gone.

Geraldine herself met them at the front door and as she led the two of them to another room that she called the parlor, Juliet marveled at all the fresh flowers sitting here and there, the antique furniture and the photos and paintings on the wall. Everything in the house seemed to have character and history to it and the images definitely brought home the fact to Juliet that Geraldine was proud of her heritage. No wonder she was reluctant to dig into the unknown past of her husband's death or that of her grandfather. She wouldn't want her family's image tarnished for any reason. And especially not for newspaper sales.

Juliet silently groaned. She didn't want to think about that tonight. She loved Matt. And his family was becoming her family, too. She was finding everything her heart had ever hungered for. What would Matt and Geraldine think if she wrote a story about their ancestors, even if it was a good story? Would they be resentful? Would they ever forgive her? Dear God, she prayed, she had to do this right. Otherwise she was going to lose everything that had ever mattered to her.

Gracia and Lex were waiting for them in the parlor and Nicci showed up within a few minutes. Cook served the adults strong margaritas in cold, fluted glasses, while Gracia had to settle for a soda over ice.

Juliet was surprised to see the teenager dressed in a skirt and short-sleeved sweater tonight. Her long hair was swept demurely back into a neat French braid and she looked far more mature than the girl that Juliet had found crying on the lawn that day of the wedding. She appeared to be far happier, too, and Juliet truly hoped that she was a part of the reason a smile was now on the teenager's face.

As for Matt, he seemed to be totally comfortable with the idea that she was sitting close beside him in the presence of his family. In fact, he took her hand often and each time he looked at her, she could feel the undercurrents of his desire throbbing through to her fingertips. The subtle glints in his eyes were tiny promises of what the night would bring, and Juliet found it a struggle to keep her mind on the conversations around them.

"Now that the house isn't full of wedding guests," she told Geraldine, "I can see just how beautiful it is."

The older woman, who was dressed casually in jeans and a checked shirt with a turquoise bolo tie fastened at her throat, looked at her and smiled warmly. "Thank you, Juliet. After we eat, I'll have Matt take you on a tour. When he was just a boy, he used to reside here, he knows all about the house."

Juliet's gaze vacillated between Geraldine and Matt. "What was that like, living with your sister and brother-in-law?" she asked the woman.

Geraldine laughed with genuine pleasure. "Oh, it was wonderful. I wouldn't trade those years for anything. Of course, Liz and I were both very young then and we had energy to spare. And believe me, we needed it with both of us chasing after young children and trying to help with chores here on the ranch, too. Paul's job required him to do a lot of entertaining so I was constantly planning parties and welcoming executives into our home." She turned a fond smile on Matt. "Mingo, Matt's father, hated all the socializing and would always find some reason to stay down at the barn until all the guests had gone."

"So now we know where he gets his antisocial attitude," Nicci teased from across the room.

"I'm not antisocial." Matt spoke up in his own defense. "I just prefer things quiet."

"Yeah, like a tomb," Lex put in.

Everyone laughed at that, including Gracia,

who was curled up on the opposite side of her father.

"Aunt Geraldine says Daddy was naughty when he was little. But he doesn't want to talk about that in front of me," she said with smiling mischief.

Juliet laughed. "I'll bet somebody around here is willing to tell on him."

"Well," Nicci said, "I have to admit that all of us kids were rather rambunctious. I'm surprised this house still looks as good as it does. We used to run up and down the staircase, skate on the floors and slide down the banister. We tried experiments in the kitchen and ended up blowing yellow food coloring all over the walls and floors. One time when we were about ten or eleven, Matt took his lariat and tied the door handle to my bedroom shut so that I couldn't get out."

Grinning, Juliet turned her head to look at him and found grooves of amusement bracketing his lips, but it was the twinkle in his eyes that told her he'd not always been a serious man.

"Always a cowboy, sounds like," she said.

"Always," Geraldine spoke up. "Matt used to howl when Liz would haul him out of the saddle and make him come in to do his homework."

Not about to be left out, Lex said to his sister, "What about me, Nicci? You didn't tell Juliet that I was the one who was your hero and came along and let you out of your bedroom. Took some doing, too. I had to get out my bowie knife and cut Matt's rope. He was mad as a hornet."

Nicci laughed. "That's why you ended up with a black eye, little brother."

The bantering and laughter continued until Cook appeared in the doorway to call them to the dining room. The group quickly made a noisy exit to that part of the house. Matt kept his arm firmly around the back of Juliet's waist and she welcomed the affectionate contact. It made her feel wanted and connected to him in a special way.

Once they gathered around the table, Gracia was quick to point out Juliet's chair, which was, of course, next to Matt's. The teenager sat on the opposite side of her.

The dining room was large, with the long walls broken up by several wide arched windows. A long table with enough room for twelve people was covered in a deep red tablecloth and set with colorful Mexican pottery. In the middle, small bowls of yellow marigolds sat at intervals to lend a festive mood to the meal.

Nearly an hour later, the steaks and accompanying dishes had been eaten and Lex was beginning to stretch.

"Great supper, Mom, but I've got several phone calls to make tonight before I turn in." As Matt's cousin rose from the table, he looked over at Juliet and gave her a smile and a wink. "Juliet, your company really brightened the place up tonight. I hope we'll see you again soon."

"Thank you," she murmured.

Once Lex had left the table Nicci quickly followed, saying she had medical reports to read. Matt said to Juliet, "If you're ready, I think we'd better be going, too."

Geraldine frowned at her nephew. "But you haven't shown Juliet the house yet. Surely you can do that before you go."

"I have to be up at four in the morning," he explained. "And Juliet has to be at work early, too. We'll do it another night, Geraldine."

The older woman smiled her concession. "I understand. Besides, that will give you a good excuse to bring Juliet back for another visit."

Nodding, Juliet quickly expressed her thanks to Geraldine for the meal and her hospitality, then rose from the table.

"If you don't mind waiting for just a minute or two," she told Matt, "I'd like to go to the kitchen and thank Cook for the lovely meal."

"Sure," he said. "I'll be waiting out on the porch."

Jumping eagerly to her feet, Gracia said to Juliet, "I'll show you the way."

The teenager grabbed Juliet's arm and practically pulled her out of the dining room, then once they entered a wide hallway, Gracia tugged her to one side.

"You probably already know the way to the kitchen," she said in a conspiring whisper, "but I wanted to talk to you without Daddy hearing."

Juliet studied the teenager's sweet, eager face. "Why? Is something wrong?"

"No! No, I think everything is cool! Daddy likes you. Really, really likes you! I can tell."

With a cautious smile, Juliet said, "Well, honey, I don't know about the really, really part. But we have become—close," she said, unable to think of a more suitable word to describe her relationship with Matt.

Gracia sighed with a mixture of joy and hope. "Oh, Juliet, wouldn't it be wonderful if you became my mother?"

Concerned now, Juliet carefully took the girl by the shoulders. "Gracia, listen to me," she said gently. "I would consider it a great honor to be your mother. You'd be everything I could ever want in a daughter. But a decision like that isn't entirely up to you and me. Your father has a say in this, too. And we all need time to think about how being a family would change our lives."

Gracia opened her mouth with plans to argue that point, then just as quickly changed her mind and gave Juliet a knowing smile. "I guess you're right. But I don't want to be old and grown-up by the time Daddy decides to get married. I want to have you for a mother now."

The idea that Gracia placed that much affection on her was enough to sting Juliet's eyes with tears. She tried to blink them away as she gave the girl a brief hug.

Clearing her throat, Juliet said, "Sure I'm right. You wouldn't want your father choosing your boyfriend, would you?"

Aghast at that idea, Gracia blurted, "No!" Then giggled with afterthought. "He'd choose some nerd who was scared of his own shadow. I'll do my own choosing."

"That's how he feels about it, too. So just be patient. And in the meantime we can enjoy seeing each other as often as we can. Okay?"

Gracia's expression turned sober and after a short nod, she flung her arms around Juliet's neck and hung on for a long moment. "I love you, Juliet. No matter what my daddy does."

Emotion swelled in Juliet's throat, forcing her to swallow several times before she could manage to speak. "And I love you, too, Gracia. No matter what."

A few minutes later, Matt and Juliet left the ranch. Throughout the drive back to town they made sporadic small talk, but for the most part Matt was quiet. By the time they reached her place, she was growing concerned that something was bothering him.

"You've been quiet, Matt," she said as he parked the truck in the front driveway to her house. "Is anything wrong?"

After switching off the motor, he turned to

her. "No. I've just been…thinking about tonight, at the ranch."

The glow of a nearby streetlamp was enough to see his pensive expression and Juliet studied it carefully as she waited and hoped for him to continue.

"It was nice having you there with my family. I never realized how much I missed having someone beside me—to share things with." With a heavy sigh, he reached for her hand. "For a long time now Lex has accused me of being dead. And I guess maybe he was right to a certain degree. I can see now how much I've cocooned myself." He lifted her fingers to his lips. "You've come along and made me see things I refused to face before, Juliet. And now—well, you've made me feel like a new man."

Shocked by his admission, she stared at him until her heart grew so full she could no longer keep her distance.

Quickly sliding across the seat, she slipped her arms around his neck and pressed her lips against the side of his neck. "Oh, Matt. You've made me feel all new, too. New and happy."

Groaning, he caught her face between his hands and brought her lips to his. He kissed her for long moments, a slow, thorough search that left her insides quivering with need.

Once he finally lifted his head, she said, "You are coming in, aren't you?"

He gently pushed his fingers through the blond waves dipping near her cheek and she turned her mouth into his palm to kiss the calloused skin.

"I shouldn't," he said ruefully. "Neither one of us has had much sleep. And we both have to work." His mouth twisted as he leaned his forehead against hers. "But I can't resist you," he whispered.

Juliet brought her lips temptingly up to his, then kissed him softly before she finally eased away from him to gather up her handbag. Matt followed her cue and the two of them quickly exited the truck. The way to the house was dimly illuminated by a streetlamp, making it fairly easy for her to find her house key.

Once inside, she didn't bother turning on a lamp. Instead, she took him by the hand and led him straight to her bedroom at the back of the house.

The green glow of an alarm clock sitting on the nightstand was the only light in the room. It was enough to direct their path to the side of the bed and after that, their hands needed no light as they quickly did away with buttons and zippers. Clothing and shoes were tossed aside and then Matt was laying her on the soft, down coverlet.

"You're the first man to ever be in this house," she whispered as he fit his naked body next to hers.

His hand paused on her shoulder and she knew her remark had surprised him.

"Don't you mean the first man to be in your bedroom?"

"No. I mean the first to be in the house entirely," she corrected as her hands hungrily began to roam his hard chest. "I haven't had a male caller. Not since I moved here from Dallas. I guess you could say I've cocooned myself, too. And all this time I've been swearing I wouldn't let another man get near me. I didn't want to get hurt again, Matt." She brought her hands to his face and stroked her fingers along his cheeks. "Please don't hurt me, Matt. That's all I ask."

Her throaty plea brought a groan from deep within him. "Oh honey, no. You don't need to worry about that. Tonight and all the nights ahead there'll be no talk of hurting. We have much better things to do."

Juliet had to agree. After all, it was way too late to be worrying about getting hurt. She was already in love with the man. The only thing she could do now was go forward and trust him to handle her heart with care.

"You're right, Matt," she whispered as she nestled her head beneath his chin. "And all evening I've been thinking about us being together again. I guess that makes me a wanton hussy, doesn't it?"

"Absolutely," he said with a chuckle.

His response lightened her dark moment and the pleasure of being in his arms took control of her senses.

Last night on the Sandbur the urgency of first coming together had made their love-making almost frantic, but tonight Matt seemed content to take things at a slower pace.

His hands took their easy time stroking, exploring, touching places that made her groan with need and writhe in search of relief, all while he whispered adoring things in her ears. He spattered kisses across her forehead, cheeks and lips, then turned his attention to her breasts.

Each rounded globe received the delicate trace of his moist tongue, the teasing nip of his teeth, until Juliet was aching with desire. Her hands gripped his shoulders, her fingers clung as she rode wave after wave of delicious heat.

"Matt," she gasped. "Matt, I can't take much more."

"Oh yes you can, baby. We're just now getting started."

With that his head made a downward descent and his lips skimmed over her midriff and across her lower belly. At the same time, his hand found the intimate folds between her thighs and then thrust a finger inside.

A low, desperate groan began to vibrate in Juliet's throat as her senses quickly spiraled out of control. She tried to hold back the powerful surges within her body. Tried to wait for each caress, each kiss. But the ache became too much and she began to cry out for relief at the same time his tongue replaced the tempting strokes of his finger.

The incredibly intimate contact instantly pushed her over the edge and she arched frantically against him as pleasure splintered her body into tiny, glowing pieces.

Above her Matt felt his loins tightening, begging to follow her to paradise. He waited until she'd caught her breath and then entered her with one desperate thrust.

The hot sweetness of her enfolded him, tightened around him like velvet bands. Her hips rose to meet his and he knew she was ready to ride another wave.

He tried to make the minutes last, to keep the ecstasy going on and on. But all too soon he was clutching her hips, driving himself into her as he lost his seed, his heart and soul.

The end was draining for both of them and long minutes passed before they could move to the middle of the bed and snuggle their bodies comfortably together.

Juliet rested her head upon his damp shoulder and wrapped her arm across his chest. The scent of his skin enveloped her and filled her with contentment. His hard body was the anchoring rock she'd often reached for but never found until now and the realization left her sighing with happiness.

"You're not going to leave now, are you?" she whispered drowsily.

His fingers skimmed across her cheek and into her hair. "No," he said huskily, then pressed his lips against her forehead. "Go to sleep, my darling."

Juliet didn't want to sleep. She wanted to savor every moment of being close to this man that she loved. But exhaustion quickly overtook her and she drifted off before she could stop herself.

Amazingly, she didn't waken until early-morning light was streaming through a nearby window. Matt was nowhere in sight and the comforter had been spread over her naked body. The scent of fresh coffee was coming from the kitchen and since her coffeemaker wasn't automatic, she knew Matt had made the brew.

She was pushing the tangled hair from her face and trying to gather enough energy to throw her legs over the side of the bed, when Matt strode into the room carrying a steaming cup.

Dressed only in jeans and boots, his smile was a little sheepish as he eased down on the edge of the bed and carefully placed the warm cup into her hands.

"I'm not very practiced at this," he said. "So I won't guarantee that it's palatable."

Juliet wasn't thinking about the taste of

the coffee as her eyes took in his broad shoulders and wide chest, the patch of furry black hair growing between his nipples. The taste of him was far more interesting. But the coffee was what he was offering her now and with a grateful smile, she took the cup and lifted it to her lips. The drink was rich and strong, just like him.

"I expect Juan is wondering why you weren't in the kitchen this morning for breakfast," she said after several careful sips. "I thought—I half expected to wake up and see that you'd left in the night."

Her eyes met his and with a gentle twist to his lips, he reached out and touched his fingers to her cheek.

"Sunshine," he murmured. "That's what you look like this morning."

Incredibly, the sweet comment caused a blush to sting her face. "You're being funny now. I know how I really look and it couldn't be good."

His face solemn, his fingertips faintly traced the hollow beneath her eye, then settled at the corner of her lips.

"I don't know how to be funny," he said. "You know that."

Her heart thudded with love and longing and she knew if she lived to be a hundred his touch would still thrill her.

"Maybe I should teach you a few jokes," she teased.

Sighing, he dropped his hand, then bent over and reached for his shirt that was lying on the floor. As he slipped his arms into the sleeves, he said, "Lex is going to forget all about joking if I don't get home. We're supposed to gather cattle this morning and I'm late. Very late."

Glancing at the clock beside the bed, Juliet saw that she had forty minutes to get ready and drive to the newspaper office. If she hurried, she could do it in fifteen. The rest of those minutes she wanted, needed to spend with him.

As he finished buttoning his shirt, Juliet placed her hand on his forearm. "What about breakfast? I thought I'd fix us something."

He cast her a rueful glance. "I'm sorry, Juliet. I'd like nothing better. But I've got to get going."

Sometime between last night and this morning, Juliet had decided she could no longer put off talking to Matt about the Ketchum article she was being forced to write. She wanted it out in the open, before their relationship went any further.

"I understand. I just—" Uncertain now, she reached for his hand and wrapped her fingers tightly around his. "There's something I've been wanting to discuss with you and I thought this morning we could—talk about it over breakfast."

A tiny frown marred his forehead. "If it's something that important to you, then we don't want to rush it through in a couple of minutes. We'll get together again soon and then you can tell me all about it. Okay?"

Juliet had to agree. Explaining her situation with Gilbert was going to take longer than two minutes. Especially if she wanted Matt to fully understand the problem.

Nodding, she did her best to hide her disappointment and put on a happy face. "Of course. It can keep."

A flash of relief crossed his face only to be instantly replaced with vague concern as he leaned earnestly toward her and threaded his free hand through her tangled hair.

"Juliet, this isn't about you and me, is it? You're still okay with the two of us being together?"

Hope, love and fear balled together and stuck in Juliet's throat. For a moment all she could do was nod, then with a little cry, she buried her face in the curve of his neck.

"Oh, Matt. It's more than okay. It's—" She swallowed, then raised her face to his. "The best thing that's ever happened to me."

Relief washed over his face and he smiled. "That's enough to keep me happy."

He placed a swift kiss on her lips, then quickly rose to his feet and stuffed the tails of his shirt into his jeans. As he raked fingers through his tousled hair and reached for his hat, Juliet wrapped the sheet around her nakedness and swung her legs over the side of the bed.

"I'll walk you to the door," she told him.

Tugging the black felt low on his forehead, he looked at Juliet and winked. "You don't need to be dressed just for that task."

Clutching the sheet to her breasts, she tried to laugh and forget about the heavy concerns in her heart.

"I think I'd better, or you and Lex will never get those cattle gathered," she teased.

"You're probably right," he teased back, then with a wicked smile, motioned for her to precede him out of the bedroom.

At the door he gave her a lengthy kiss, then left the house without any more words of parting.

Her heart full, Juliet watched him until he climbed into his truck and drove away. But once she moved away from the door and walked back into the bedroom where they'd shared such deep intimacies, her mind quickly began to spin with doubts.

Maybe she was the reason he'd woken from a deep sleep and started to live again. He certainly seemed interested in reviving his sex life. But none of that necessarily meant he could ever love her. And even if he could, would writing the Ketchum article wipe all his feelings for her away?

Unfortunately, the answer to that was going to have to be pushed aside until they met again.

Chapter Eleven

Mingo Sanchez used both hands to outline the shape of a curvy woman in the open space in front of his wheelchair, then turned questioning eyes on Matt.

Normally, Matt was here at the Sunset Manor to pick up Gracia from her regular visit of Bible reading with her grandfather. But today she'd come home from school with a bit of a sore throat and neither one of them had wanted to expose Mingo to any unnecessary germs that might give him a setback. So instead of hearing his granddaughter read the

Bible, Mingo had been sitting and listening to his eldest son struggling with the retelling of Job's miseries.

But after twenty minutes, the older Sanchez had made it plain he knew enough about trials and tribulations and had turned his attention away from the Good Book.

Cocking a suspect brow at his father, Matt said, "Are you asking me about Juliet Madsen?"

The older man smiled broadly and nodded, then reached for the paper and pencil lying ready on his lap.

After a slow struggle, one word began to emerge. Date.

Matt said the word aloud and Mingo smiled and pointed at his son. The meaning was very clear.

Knowing there was no use in avoiding the matter with his father, Matt nodded. "Yes, Juliet and I have gone on more than one date. I guess that makes you happy, doesn't it?"

With another grin, Mingo nodded, then as quick as his struggling hand could, he scratched out another word. Love.

For a moment Matt was taken aback by his father's question. Even when he'd been a healthy man, Mingo had liked to tease both his sons about women and sex. But when it came to the more serious emotion, he'd always kept his questions and opinions to himself, unless his sons sought out his advice. Matt was surprised to see his father break his own rule this time.

"Do I love her? Dad, it's too soon to be asking me something like that. I like her very much. That's a start, isn't it?"

Even as he said the words to his father, Matt felt like a fraud of sorts. *Like* wasn't nearly a strong enough word to describe his feelings for Juliet. But love? He didn't want to think his heart had ventured that far out on a limb, so far that he might never be able to yank it back from a fall. Yet he was beginning to wonder and ask himself if this desperate need he felt for the woman was something akin to that emotion. Three days had passed since he'd kissed Juliet goodbye at her house and he was already desperately hungry to see her again.

Mingo frowned at him with obvious disapproval and Matt sighed.

"Dad, a man isn't supposed to just jump straight into the fire. He needs to ask himself if he can stand the heat, first."

Mingo rolled his eyes and Matt knew he wasn't fooling his father or himself. He'd already jumped straight into the flames with Juliet.

"All right," Matt said crossly. "I'm crazy about the woman. But I don't know if what I'm feeling is love. And you don't, either."

His expression clearly full of disgust, his father simply stared at him. Matt wanted to throw up his hands and walk out of the room. But he didn't. Mingo needed his son just as much as Matt needed his father.

With a heavy sigh, Matt rose from the stool he'd angled up to his father's wheelchair, then walked to the head of the bed and carefully placed the Bible where his father could easily reach it.

Once he turned back around Mingo had something else to say and Matt watched dumbfounded as his father pointed to the wedding band on his finger, then folded his arms and made a motion as though he were rocking a baby.

"Married! A baby!" he muttered with disbelief. "Dad, take a look at me! I'm nearly forty years old. It's too late for me to be starting over again."

This time Matt's response made Mingo so angry, he motioned for him to leave the room.

Matt said sharply, "All right. I'm going. But first we have to talk about these tests you're going to take next week." Walking over to his father, he looked down at him. "Do you still want to go through the long trip to Houston and then have all those doctors and nurses poking and prodding you?"

His lips clamped in a crooked line, Mingo nodded.

"And what if the tests say there's nothing the doctors can do? I don't want you to slip into a depression. And if they do decide to try an operation, it could be dangerous. Really dangerous," Matt couldn't help but warn. The thought of losing his father was too frightful to bear.

Mingo's dark eyes searched his son's face keenly before he once again wrote on the paper. *Look at me.*

Matt did as his father ordered and the sight very nearly broke his heart. One leg was useless and one arm so weak it was close to being worthless. He couldn't talk or even eat the foods he wanted to eat. This was not the way his strong, vibrant father wanted to live and Matt couldn't expect him to simply sit there and play things safe.

With a lump in his throat, Matt squeezed his father's shoulders. "I know, Dad. I don't want you like this, either. But I'm selfish. And I don't want to lose you."

With a vague smile, Mingo patted his hand, then wrote one last word. *Faith.*

Yeah, how many times had Matt told himself to have faith, only to have his world torn asunder, he wondered. If faith was ever going to bring him a happy ending, it was sure slow in coming.

A few minutes later, after Matt left the nursing home in his truck, he decided to drive by the newspaper building and see if Juliet was still there at work.

For the past three days he'd been trying to find a moment to call her, but one thing after another had popped up on the ranch and he'd fallen into bed late each night. This evening he was determined to see her and talk with her, even if it meant driving to her house.

Ever since he'd learned that he would be taking his father to Houston next week, he'd dallied with the idea of inviting Juliet to go with him. He had no idea if she could be away from her work for that long, but he was hoping she could manage it somehow. He needed her company and her support and he wasn't going to be bashful about telling her so.

The parking spaces allotted for the newspaper workers were located in an alley behind the back of a row of buildings. Juliet's small car was parked there among several other vehicles, so he was safe in assuming she was still working.

He found a space to park, then entered a single back door of the newspaper office. The scent of ink and chemicals met his nose as he walked into what appeared to be a large room where the printing presses were located.

A young man loading bundles of flyers onto a crate happened to look around and spot him. Matt waited for the young man to approach him.

"Looking for someone?" he asked.

Matt nodded. "Sorry I came in the back," he apologized. "I'm looking for Juliet Madsen. Can I get to her office from here?"

The young man nodded. "Sure. Follow me and I'll show you."

After a few twists and turns through double

doors and down several corridors, the man gestured to an open door with Juliet's name plaque hanging on it.

"This is Ms. Madsen's office. Looks like she's not in at the moment, but she will be. Just have a seat and wait."

Trusting boy, Matt thought wryly, as he stepped into the small room and took a seat in a chair near Juliet's desk.

After making himself comfortable, Matt looked curiously around the space where Juliet worked. It was cluttered with an assortment of things, including boxes of files and papers lining the edges of the walls. More papers, along with an array of pens, highlighters, a large atlas and legal pads were piled upon her L-shaped desk. A foam cup, half-full of coffee was sitting near a mouse pad. Since it lacked any steam, Matt figured the drink had long ago grown cold. In an opposite corner from where he was sitting, high upon a shelf, a tiny radio was tuned in to a station that played standards. At the moment a man was singing about walking on the street where his lover lived and how just being near her transformed his world into a magical place.

The lyrics could have been describing him, Matt decided. Just having Juliet in his life had changed his very way of thinking. The sun was brighter and hotter, the sky bluer and good food even better. That blissful notion had him suddenly thinking about his father's serious suggestion about Matt marrying Juliet and having a child. And for the first time since Erica had died, Matt wondered if he really could start over. Would Juliet want to marry him? Have children with him?

The questions were not something he'd ever thought he'd want to contemplate. But now they filled him with excitement, an eagerness for the future that he'd lost so long ago.

Restless now for Juliet to appear, he rose from the chair and began to move impatiently around the room. After a moment, he paused at a large map of the Republic of Texas hanging on one wall and studied the geography. Eventually, he grew bored with that and drifted back toward her desk.

It was then Matt noticed the papers stacked at the far end of the desk and a measurable distance from her computer screen. The papers were photocopies of old newspapers from the past and one of the headlines glared up at him. Murder on the Sandbur.

Wondering how he could have missed seeing the paper when he'd first entered the office, he snatched it up and quickly scanned the information from a 1962 edition of the *Fannin Review*. The article was the first of many that had been written about his grandfather's untimely death.

Matt didn't bother reading the piece. Instead, he began to flip through the other photocopies and as he did, his heart began to sink right down to his feet. All of the papers were pertaining to his grandparents, Nate and Sara Ketchum. Which could only mean one thing. Juliet was researching his family's history with the intentions of writing a story, *the* story that she'd been planning from that very first appearance she'd made at Raine's wedding.

How could he have been so stupid, so gullible? He'd believed her when she'd assured him she would never do anything to hurt his family. What did she think this was going to do, make them all happy?

Gritting his teeth, he started to slam the papers back down on the desk, but the sound of a footstep caused him to pause and look up.

Juliet rounded the doorway, then stopped in her tracks when she spotted Matt standing near her desk. His face was pale and rigid and the papers he gripped between both fists clearly explained the reason for his strained expression.

With a sick feeling swimming in her stomach, she stepped forward. "Hello, Matt. I didn't know you were here, someone should have paged me."

His lips twisted to a sneer. "So you could have hidden these from my sight?" He shook the papers at her. "Why are these stories about my grandparents on your desk, Juliet? Can you tell me something—anything that will make me believe you haven't been lying to me?"

The stricken look on his face made her want to drop her face in her hands and weep, but that would do nothing to help the situation, so she straightened her shoulders and walked over to him.

"I haven't been lying to you, Matt. I told you that I would never write anything salacious or misleading about your family. And I'm not. That—" she pointed to the papers still clutched in his fists "—is only research."

Anger suddenly burned in his eyes and he

tossed the photocopies toward the desk. Some of them landed. Others simply floated to the floor. Matt ignored them and so did she.

"Why, Juliet? Why would you do such a thing? Is getting a story all you've ever cared about? Am I supposed to believe that you haven't been insinuating yourself into my family just for this?"

He pounded a finger on her desk and each angry thump fired her temper to a higher degree. How dare he mistrust her, she thought, after all that they'd shared, after he'd vowed to always trust her, to never hurt her. How could he be so quick to believe the worst?

Moving closer, she jabbed her finger in the middle of his chest. "I haven't been insinuating myself into any part of your family! I was invited, remember?"

"God help me, I wish I could forget!" he shot back at her.

"Matt, you're jumping to conclusions. The wrong conclusions. If you'll let me explain—"

"Explain what?" he interrupted sharply. "That you weren't planning on writing a story about my grandparents?"

Shaking her head, she dropped her finger

from his chest and wiped a shaky hand through her tousled hair. "No. I'm not going to tell you that. I'm going to tell you that Gilbert is still demanding that I do this story."

His eyes widened with such a look of fury that Juliet feared he was going to run out of the office and go after the man with his bare hands.

"Then tell him to go to hell!" he yelled.

Figuring every office down the hall could hear the two of them quarreling, Juliet hurried to shut the door before she faced him again.

"I can't do that, Matt," she said calmly. "This is my job. Writing stories is what I do. I didn't claw my way through college just to quit when I run up against a stubborn editor."

"Not even for me?"

The simple question stabbed her deeply and for a moment she wanted to give in, to tell him that she'd do exactly what he wanted. She'd tell Gilbert she was leaving. But in the end she understood that quitting or running wouldn't fix things. Eventually she would resent the fact that Matt wouldn't or couldn't trust her to do the right thing. Moreover, Gilbert would simply find someone else to do the story and the next person might not be as kind toward the Sandbur families as she would be.

"Matt," she said gently, "I would give up this job in a minute if I thought it would fix all this between us. But it won't."

His face like stone, he shook his head. "Seven years I've done without a woman and now you've come along and made a fool out of me. I thought—you cared, Juliet."

Her heart was drowning in tears as she reached out and touched a hand to his chest. "I do care, Matt. More than you know. I love you. I love you and Gracia."

His head actually reared back on her last words and when he finally spoke, his voice was dripping with scorn. "Do you honestly think I'd believe something like that now?"

Not waiting for her answer, he started toward the door. Juliet followed and snared a hold on his arm before he could twist the knob.

"Matt, running out isn't going to help." She tried to reason with him. "And for your information I tried to talk to you about this matter before. The other morning before you left my house, I told you I wanted to discuss something with you. Well, this is it. So you see, I wasn't going to do anything behind your back."

His eyes looked right through her as

though she were the floor and he wanted to simply step over her.

"It doesn't make any difference if you were going to tell me about this then or now. You've made your choice and it wasn't me."

He reached to open the door and she stubbornly tugged on his arm again. This time when he looked at her she was angry and barely able to control her tears.

Her voice low and shaky, she said, "I believed you cared about me, Matt. I thought you cared enough to trust me—about this— about everything. But you didn't. All I've been to you is a bed partner."

His jaw tight, he turned away from the door to stare accusingly at her. "I came by here this evening to invite you to go to Houston with me and my father. He's going into the hospital for several tests and I wanted you to be there with me—with us. Now I'm glad I didn't mention my intentions to him. I'll wait until he's through all this before I burst his bubble about you."

Jerking open the door, Matt left the office before Juliet could say anything. But even if he hadn't stormed out, she doubted she could have made any sort of reply. She felt crushed and so sick it was all she could do to make it over to her desk chair and drop her head in her hands.

A week and a half later, Matt was sitting in a Houston hospital cafeteria, trying his best to eat a sandwich, but finding it impossible to swallow more than half of the cold tuna.

He'd been here with his father for four long days. The isolation from the ranch, along with anxiety over Mingo's tests was getting to him. Not to mention the devastation he felt every time he thought of Juliet. And that was at least twenty-three hours of every day.

Dear God, he was an utter mess. He couldn't eat, think or sleep. He'd been moving through each day in a fog of misery. He functioned, but only out of necessity. And he was beginning to wonder if he'd ever be normal again.

Before he'd left the Sandbur for the trip here to Houston, Juliet had called and pleaded with him to see her so that they could try to talk things out between them. Just hearing her voice over the telephone had cracked his heart all over again. He'd told her he never wanted to see her again and hung up the phone. Since then he'd had no more contact with her and that was just the way he wanted it.

The woman had duped him, defied him and made a fool of him. So why was he still aching for her?

"Excuse me, Mr. Sanchez, I hate to interrupt your meal, but would you mind if I joined you?"

The male voice interrupted Matt's black thoughts and he looked up to see Mingo's doctor standing at the edge of the small round table. The sight of the neurosurgeon sent a shaft of fear through Matt's already troubled heart. He'd already lost so many of the people he loved. How could he bear to lose another?

Matt gestured toward the chair opposite him. "Please do. Is anything wrong?"

The young doctor gave him a brief smile. "No. Not exactly. I just came from your father's room and I wanted to discuss with you what the two of us talked about. Mr. Sanchez told me you were down here eating so I took the chance that I'd find you."

Matt released a pent-up breath. "I'm glad. You can probably guess that I've been on pins and needles, wondering about the results of Dad's tests. Do you have them now?"

The doctor nodded. "I do. And I've conferred with three other doctors here on staff. They all agree with me that your father's condition might be reversed with surgery."

Matt's jaw dropped with surprise. This was the last thing he'd expected to hear and he suddenly realized how negatively he'd viewed his father's future. "Reversed? You mean my father might be well again—like his old self?"

Folding his arms across his chest, the doctor studied Matt carefully. "That's what I'm saying. Of course he would need a lot of rehabilitation after the surgery to get to that point. But I think it's possible. And your father is willing to work."

Matt darted an anxious look at the man. "I hear a *but* in there somewhere. What haven't you told me?"

"The surgery would be risky. If things didn't go right, his condition could worsen or he could even die. If you'd like to come to my office, I can show you the brain scans and explain it to you better in medical terms."

Shaking his head, Matt said, "There's no need for that, doctor. All that matters is what my father wants."

"He wants the surgery. He wants the chance to be a whole man again. As soon as possible. So I've scheduled the surgery for the morning. If there are other family members who want to be here, you ought to contact them today."

Matt nodded numbly and the doctor went on to explain a bit more about the surgery before he finally rose and left the table with an encouraging word.

Once the neurosurgeon was gone, Matt swallowed down the last of his soda and hurried to his father's room.

The moment Matt rounded the door and Mingo spotted his son, the older man's face split into a wide smile and with his most flexible hand, he motioned for Matt to come to the bedside.

"I just saw the doctor, Dad. He's told me about the surgery." His throat tight, he reached over and rubbed a hand over Mingo's curly hair. "Guess you're all excited about it."

A smile still creasing his face, Mingo nodded, then tapped a finger to the scar on his head before he finally made an okay sign with his thumb and forefinger.

Matt did his best to smile back at his father.

"Yeah, Dad, I know you've always told me you were going to get well. I guess I should have listened to you." The smile fell from his face as he reached for his father's hand and gripped it tightly. "I know you want this chance, Dad. And I guess I want it for you. But what the hell am I going to do if something happens to you?"

With a serene expression, Mingo tapped his wedding band, then pointed toward the blue sky beyond the window. Matt didn't have to ask more. It was obvious his father would be just as happy to meet up with his wife in heaven. To Mingo, this was a win-win situation.

"Yes, Mother's out there waiting for you. But she doesn't mind waiting, cause she knows how much we all need you. Especially Gracia. She's been calling twice a day, wanting to know when you're coming home. She's always believed that you're going to walk and talk again. Guess you're going to prove your granddaughter right," Matt added soberly.

With another big smile, Mingo nodded, then his expression changed to one of concern as he studied Matt's glum face. Finally, he pointed to his son's empty ring finger and raised his brows in question.

Matt heaved out a heavy sigh. "I don't want to talk about that, Dad. Juliet and I—well, I'm not seeing her anymore."

Why? The question was shouting from Mingo's eyes.

Matt dropped his father's hand and turned away from the bed. "We—uh, had an argument," he muttered. "I found out she was going to do something that I didn't want her to do."

He walked around the sparse hospital room as precious memories of Juliet bombarded him from all directions. Her smile and scent, the touch of her hands and the sweet give of her body haunted his every waking hour. How could he ever forget and move beyond what they'd shared together?

Looking up, Matt realized he'd circled the room and was now back beside his father's bed. Apparently while he'd been mentally torturing himself, his father had been writing on the pad by his side. Now he motioned for Matt to read.

Liz made me angry. Love all that matters.

Love? Was that what this aching need in Matt's chest was, he wondered. Is that why he couldn't forget? Why he couldn't envision his future without Juliet in it? He'd felt for a long time that he loved Juliet, but not until this moment had he found the courage to really admit it openly to himself.

Matt looked helplessly at his father and Mingo began to slowly scratch out another message.

Just watching his father's shaky hand struggle to work the pencil intensified the importance Mingo put behind his words.

Precious time.

To emphasize his meaning, Mingo touched his wedding band, his heart, then finally pointed toward heaven.

Matt felt the sting of tears at the back of his eyes. His father knew what it was like to love, really love. He was telling Matt not to waste precious time. And suddenly he realized that Juliet going behind his back, or writing the article was not the real reason he'd broken their relationship. Deep down, he'd been afraid of losing her, just as he'd lost Erica, and his mother, and other dear members of his family. But now his father was telling him to live and love and not waste precious time. Did he have the courage?

Reaching for the cell phone in his pocket,

he said, "I'd better call the family and let them know about your surgery."

Mingo shook his head and quickly made an hourglass shape with his hands to signify Juliet. Apparently he was more concerned about Matt contacting Juliet than he was the rest of the family.

Matt sighed. "I don't know, Dad. I'll think about calling her later."

Mingo gave him a weary smile, then an okay sign with his thumb and forefinger.

Chapter Twelve

More than a week later Juliet was sitting in the Cattle Call ignoring the salad in front of her when Angie popped down in the seat next to her.

"Is something wrong with the food, Juliet? If the salad isn't any good, I'll have the cook make you another one."

Sighing, Juliet shook her head and poked the tines of her fork halfheartedly at the lettuce and tomato. "There's nothing wrong with the food, Angie. I'm just not hungry today. I really don't even know why I walked down here. Just to get out of the office, I suppose."

The young waitress thoughtfully studied her friend's glum face. "You look horrible. In fact, you've looked horrible for the past few days. Has something happened?"

Juliet's lips twisted wryly. "Angie, you remember when we talked about the wedding I went to at the Sandbur and you were wondering what it must be like to be a part of that family?"

Her face wrinkled with confusion, Angie nodded. "Yes, I remember. What has that got to do with anything?"

Stabbing her fork into the bowl of salad, Juliet said, "I just got reminded a few days ago that I—" She looked at Angie and shrugged "—don't fit in with people like them, either."

Sympathy filled Angie's eyes as she looked at her friend. "Well, that's nothing to be sad about, Juliet. Sometimes fairy tales aren't what they're cracked up to be anyway."

"That's certainly the truth," Juliet muttered, then looked around with surprise as she saw Nicci Saddler approaching her table.

"Hello, you two," she greeted warmly.

"Dr. Saddler, how nice to see you." Angie jumped to her feet and shook the woman's hand.

"How's that sweet little girl of yours, Angie?"

Angie's face beamed and Juliet realized that even though her friend had very little monetarily, she was very rich otherwise. At least she had a child and the two of them were a family. Juliet had no one.

"She's giving the babysitter lots of trouble, so that means she's doing great. Thanks to you," Angie said, then quickly excused herself as she spotted a customer motioning for service. "I'll be back to take your order."

"Don't bother," Nicci said to the waitress. "I'm only here to talk to Juliet."

Angie hurried away and Nicci gestured to the chair the waitress had vacated.

"Mind if I sit down?"

"Of course not. It's good to see you." Juliet's mind was suddenly spinning, wondering why Matt's cousin had shown up today. She'd not heard from him or any of the family since her break with Matt, which had only reinforced the fact that her relationship with him was truly over. Even Gracia must have turned against her.

The other woman settled herself in the seat, then smiled across the table at Juliet. "Well, I thought about calling you at the newspaper office. But I decided I'd rather talk to you in person and I took a chance you'd be having lunch here today."

"I have lunch here every day," Juliet admitted with a shrug. "It's better than having bologna at my desk."

"The food must not be too good today. It doesn't look like you've eaten a thing."

Juliet's gaze dropped to the salad bowl. "Oh, you know how it is, doctor, things that are good for you don't taste good. I should have ordered a cheeseburger."

Nicci laughed softly and Juliet glanced up at her. The woman seemed unusually chipper, which only made Juliet wonder even more about her sudden appearance here in the café.

"It's good to see you, Juliet. We've all missed seeing you on the ranch."

Tears were suddenly pouring from Juliet's heart. "You mean you and your mother, don't you?"

"Well, there's Gracia, too. She's been dying to contact you."

Surprise widened Juliet's eyes. "She has? Then why hasn't she called me? Because Matt forbade her to call me?" she asked bitterly.

Nicci shook her head. "No. Because Mother and I talked her out of it. We didn't want her to be begging and pleading and putting you in an awkward position. We convinced her to wait until her father has made things right with you before she called."

Dazed by Nicci's suggestion, Juliet stared at the woman. "Then she'll be waiting for the rest of her life. Matt and I are finished. I figured you—everybody on the ranch knew that."

"Is that the way you want things to be?"

Did the woman have to ask, Juliet wondered. Couldn't she see the misery on her face? "No. But Matt is—"

"Stubborn. We all know that. But give him time. Things have been very hectic for our family these past couple of weeks. Mingo has had surgery and—"

"Mingo had surgery!" Juliet leaned eagerly toward the other woman. "What happened? How is he?"

Nicci smiled broadly. "Mingo is on the

mend. Literally. A neurosurgeon in Houston operated on his brain and repaired the damage. There's a good chance that he's going to be well again."

Joy shot through Juliet and she grabbed Nicci's hand and squeezed it tightly. "You mean he'll be able to walk and talk again?" she asked excitedly.

"With lots of rehab. But that will be a small price to pay."

Juliet stared at her in amazement. "It's a miracle."

"We all agree. But the surgery was very tedious and Mingo could have died at any moment. It was all so stressful on the family and Matt refused to leave his father for even a minute. He's just now gotten home to the ranch."

So Matt had been gone all this time, she thought. Was that the reason she'd not heard from him? No. No matter what had been going on with Mingo, he could have taken a minute or two to pick up the telephone and speak to her. And the last words he'd said to her were that he never wanted to see her again. She had to believe he meant it.

"What about Mingo? Where is he now?"

"At a rehab center in Victoria. The nurses are taking great care of him and the place is close enough for all of us to visit while he gets well."

"I'm so glad. This is such good news. Thank you for coming by to tell me."

With a wan smile, Nicci patted her hand. "I had selfish reasons. I want you in the family. So does Matt—he just hasn't realized it yet."

Swallowing at the lump in her throat, Juliet looked away from the woman and stared unseeingly at the diners scattered across the room. "Matt hates me for writing a story about his grandparents. And maybe he should. But the story isn't going to be like he thinks. But that—that won't matter to him."

"Oh, Juliet," Nicci said with a groan. "This story about Sara and Nate—it has nothing to do with Matt's anger, not really. All sorts of yarns and chronicles have been written about our grandparents. Good and bad. Ultimately, none of them have hurt any of us. We're still the same family we always were. Matt will eventually realize this. But in the meantime, maybe it would help if you tried to talk to him."

Sighing, Juliet looked at her. "I've been asking myself if it would help, or if he would even agree to see me. If he turned me away, I'm not sure I could stand it."

"At least you'd know you tried." Nicci rose from her seat and patted Juliet's shoulder. "I've got to run. We'll talk again soon."

Juliet watched the other woman leave the café, then glanced at her watch. Her lunch hour was nearly over and it was essential that she get back to her office on time.

She'd handed the Ketchum piece in to Gilbert and now, good or bad, she had to deal with the editor's reaction.

Back at the newspaper office, Juliet entered the building through the back door and walked quickly to her private workspace. She was putting her handbag away and glancing to see if anyone had left a note on her desk, when she heard a footfall.

Glancing around she saw Gilbert striding toward her. The typed papers she'd given him were in his hand and he was staring at her over the glasses perched on the end of his nose.

"Mr. Gilbert, you should have called me over the intercom and I would have walked down to your office," she suggested.

He waved a dismissive hand at her. "No need. I'm on my way to a meeting with the

Chamber of Commerce." He tossed the papers down on her desk, then folded his arms across his chest as he continued to study her. "That piece is not what I expected out of you, Madsen. I guess you know that, don't you?"

She drew in a bracing breath. "Honestly, I knew exactly the sort of story you wanted me to write. But I took a chance that you would view this thing with an open mind." She scooped up the papers and held them with the respect she felt the story deserved. "While I was researching the family, I realized that so many pieces had been written about them, but none had really focused on their lives in relation to our community or what they contributed to this whole area as ranchers and philanthropists. No one had delved into their personal relationship, other than to throw around the words adultery and murder."

Gilbert grimaced. "You've portrayed them as a loving couple."

Not about to let him intimidate her, Juliet straightened her shoulders. "That's right. From what I can gather, they were wildly in love with each other. Their four children reinforce that notion. I'll admit their marriage appeared to be stormy at times and I've expressed that in my story, but I also say that their devotion to each other kept them together."

"Hmph. Well, you also insinuate that someone else killed Nate Ketchum. Not his wife. Can you substantiate any of that theory?"

"Maybe. Right now it's more of an intuition than anything. But if I had a chance to dig more, I actually think I could find something to corroborate the assumption. Why?" she couldn't help asking.

Juliet was suddenly stunned to see something like a smile cross the man's face.

"Because I like your piece, Madsen. And I think readers will be intrigued by it. I'd like you to do more on the murder mystery. Play up the fact that you're searching for the truth and not what people around here have always assumed happened to the rancher."

She couldn't have been more surprised. "You mean that?"

He snorted out something close to a chuckle. "I'm not necessarily a great newspaper editor, Madsen. When I walked into this job I was walking backward. But I'm smart enough to know that you're good. Good enough to open my eyes." He gestured to the papers in her hands. "We'll run that in

next week's edition. In the meantime, use all
the time you need for research."

Dazed, she watched the editor turn to
leave. "Thank you, Mr. Gilbert," she called
after him. "Thank you very much."

Later that evening, on her way home,
Juliet realized she should be singing and
shouting with happy relief. Her long
labored story had not only pleased Gilbert,
but had seemed to make him do an about-
face. The man was human after all and
hopefully would be easier to work with in
the future.

Yet none of this gave her joy. She was
relieved the issue with Gilbert had been
resolved, but she was feeling nothing
remotely close to happy. What good was her
writing, her job, if she didn't have someone
to share it with, someone to be proud of her
accomplishments? What good was anything
in life without someone to love?

Matt. Oh, Matt. Her heart cried his name
as tears blurred her vision. She loved him so.
Missed him so. If she could only make him
understand how deeply she felt about him,
she thought. If only she could make him see

that he could trust her completely. But how? And would he even care enough to listen?

She didn't know the answers, but it was obvious she had to try. Moving to Goliad and falling in love with Matt had taught her that she was finished with running. She'd run from Dallas to forget her disastrous relationship with Michael and she had forgotten him. She'd even come to realize that what she'd felt for her ex-fiancé was shallow compared to the deep feelings she had for Matt. Running to the ends of the earth would never make her forget him or erase the love in her heart. The only choice she had now was to stand and fight for what she wanted the most, a family with Matt and Gracia.

Coming to that decision, Juliet wiped the moisture from her eyes and stepped down harder on the accelerator. As soon as she arrived home she was going to change clothes and head straight to the Sandbur. Whether he liked it or not, Matt was going to see her again.

She was so intent on her plans that when she rounded the last curve to her house, she didn't notice the truck parked beneath the tree in her front yard until she'd stopped her car and climbed out.

The sight of Matt's vehicle froze her in her tracks and she looked dazedly from it to the front door of the house. He wasn't in the truck or on the porch, and since she'd not bothered to lock her house this morning, that could only mean he was inside, waiting for her.

Her heart beating wildly in her chest, Juliet put one foot in front of the other until she was through the front door.

The living room was empty so she walked purposely toward the kitchen and the faint scent of coffee. By the time she reached the small room, her legs were shaking and her face had gone pale.

Matt was sitting at the small dinette, his hands wrapped around a coffee mug. Over by the cabinet counter, her Persian cat was licking at a saucer filled with cream. The idea that he'd bothered to care for her pet nearly made her burst into tears.

"He seemed to be hungry so I gave him a little half-and-half," he said of the cat.

"He's always hungry."

She moved toward the table and he said, "I found the door unlocked. I hope you don't mind me making myself at home."

Still dazed, Juliet stared at him. He was

dressed in a blue chambray work shirt with dusty jeans and boots. An equally dusty straw hat covered his black hair and shaded his eyes. He looked as though he'd just stepped out of the feedlot. But most of all, he looked downright wonderful to her aching heart.

"Of course not. Uh—have you been here long?"

With a brief shake of his head, he said, "No. Just long enough to make the coffee. I—er—I took it for granted that you wouldn't be working late this evening and came here instead of dropping by the newspaper office."

Her mind spinning, she eased the leather duffel bag off her shoulder and let it drop to the tabletop. Then running her hands nervously down her hips, she said, "I finished up at regular quitting time this evening and I—"

So many questions suddenly bottled up in her throat that she couldn't say anything else and she quickly drew in a deep breath and turned toward the cabinets. Why was he here? To put the final end to their relationship?

Her hands were shaking as she reached for a cup and filled it with some of the coffee that he'd made. She was reaching blindly for the refrigerator door with intentions of getting cream, when he suddenly rose from his seat and caught her by the arm.

Her blue eyes lifted uncertainly to his face and her heart jerked with fear at the solemn gravity she saw in his eyes.

"That can wait," he said hoarsely. "Right now I have some things I want to say to you."

Twisting around, she faced him while her heart pounded like a wild thing in her chest. "I have things I want to say to you, too. In fact, I was planning to drive out to the ranch this evening. But now—you've saved me the trip. I guess you wanted to tell me about Mingo?"

His hand slipped up her bare arm until his fingers were curled around her shoulder. The contact filled her with yearning.

"You've heard about my father?"

Nodding, she smiled in spite of her trembling nerves. "I ran into Nicci at the Cattle Call today. She says Mingo is going to be well again. I can't tell you how happy that news has made me."

A wry smile twisted his lips. "Yeah, it's made us all happy. Lucita and Marti have come home to spend time with him. And Gracia is on top of the world. She's dancing on her toes, begging to go see him. I told her to be patient and maybe you'd be willing to make the trip over to Victoria with us."

He said the words so casually that for a moment they didn't click with Juliet. When they did, she stared at him in wonder.

"*I* would go with you?" she repeated in disbelief. "You're asking me to go with you and Gracia to visit Mingo?"

Heaving out a heavy breath, he brought his other hand up to her face and Juliet felt her shaky legs threaten to buckle completely as his fingers traced a loving pattern upon her cheek.

"I'm asking. No, I'm begging, Juliet."

Begging? Matt Sanchez was begging her? Incredulous, she shook her head back and forth.

"I don't understand, Matt. You—told me over the phone that you didn't want to ever see me again. Now you're here inviting me on a family trip. I—"

His dark features suddenly crumpled with remorse. "Juliet, please forgive me for that—for every stupid thing I've said and done these past three weeks. I realize saying I'm sorry isn't enough, but just give me a chance to make things right between us."

Tears rushed to her eyes and then with a little cry she fell forward against his chest.

"Oh, Matt, Matt. I love you. I love you. Don't you realize that by now?"

Wrapping his arms around her, he buried his face in her hair and crushed her tightly against him. "Oh God, Juliet, I don't deserve you. I've been so stubborn, so narrow-minded. When I found those papers about my grandparents, all I could think was that I'd fallen in love with a woman who'd been slipping behind my back, doing things without making me a part of them—just like Erica."

Clinging to him, Juliet mouthed against his shoulder. "I thought you were angry because you believed I was going to write something salacious about them. But I wasn't. I was trying to tell you that whatever I wrote about the Ketchums would be as fair and true as I could make it be."

Easing his head back, he lifted her chin and looked at her with regret. "I wanted to believe the worst about you, Juliet. I wanted to think you were deceptive like Erica, that you were only out for a sensational story at the expense of my family. I think if this hadn't happened between us, I would have eventually looked for something else to rip us apart. Because I was scared."

His admission caused her blue eyes to widen with wonder. "Scared?"

He nodded soberly. "The more we were together, the more I realized I was falling in love with you. And the more I loved, the more scared I got." Closing his eyes, he brought his lips against her cheek. "Everybody sees me as a rich man, Juliet. And I guess in lots of ways I am. But the things that matter most I've lost. Erica, my mother, and then Dad's ordeal. I'd lost all faith that anything good and lasting could happen to me. I felt like if I loved you, I'd only wind up losing you. So I guess I unconsciously thought that I'd split us up before that could happen."

"Oh, Matt, I don't know what to say," she whispered, her voice thick with emotion. "Except that I love you. And I want us to be together for as long as we have on this earth. We don't know how long that will be. No one does. But while we're together we're going to live and love every moment."

Leaning his head back, he gave her a wry smile. "You sound like Dad. While we were in Houston, he told me I was wasting time when I could be loving you. What he said woke me up, Juliet. Seeing him there in that hospital bed and knowing he could die in surgery, yet seeing his courage to face the future, made me take a good look at myself. At what I was doing to the both of us."

Reaching up, she cupped his face with her palms. "Your father is a wise man, my darling. I'm looking forward to knowing him."

His lips spread into a seductive smile. "What about becoming his daughter-in-law?"

Joy spilled from her heart and splashed through her body like golden raindrops. "Oh, Matt, I want to be your wife. More than anything. But I think—"

She eased out of his arms and went over to the table where she'd dropped her bag. Frowning, Matt followed.

"What are you doing?" he asked as she opened the bag and pulled out a manila folder. "I just asked you to marry me and you're looking at papers?"

Turning to face him, she solemnly handed him the folder. "Before I say yes, I want you to read this. It's the story I've written about your grandparents. Gilbert plans to publish it in next week's edition."

Shaking his head, he thrust it back at her. "Whatever this says doesn't matter, Juliet. My grandparents' lives have come and gone. Their time together was passionate, mysterious and full of controversy. None of that can be changed and I've decided that I'm not going to let this change anything between us now."

Love shining in her eyes, she said, "I'm relieved that you feel that way, Matt. But I want you to read it anyway. Just so you can tell me what you think."

A smile of indulgence crossed his face and buffered his sigh of impatience. "All right. I'll read. But only because you want me to."

Juliet took him by the arm and urged him back to the chair he'd been sitting in when she'd first walked into the kitchen.

"You sit and I'll warm your coffee," she told him.

Ten minutes passed before he finally put the typed pages down and looked over to where she was standing by the cabinet counter, watching and waiting for his response.

"What do you think?" she asked softly.

Slowly, he rose from the chair and went to her. A look of amazing admiration was on his face as he clasped his hands with hers. "I think," he whispered tenderly, "that you're wonderful. More wonderful than this stubborn ole cowboy deserves."

Laughing softly, she rose on tiptoe and brought her lips up to his. "Fifty years from now I'm going to remind you of those words."

He kissed her for long, long moments, then with a wicked growl, he picked her up in his arms. And as his strong legs carried her to the bedroom, he whispered, "Then I'd better give you something else to remember with them."

Epilogue

Almost a year later, a spring sun was shining down on the Sandbur ranch, bathing the grass and new leaves with warmth, and urging the Texas bluebonnets to raise their heads.

Out in the long cattle pen, Gracia was aboard Traveler, her long ponytail bouncing wildly as the horse dived back and forth in front of the little brown steer that was trying his best to get by the horse and rider.

A short distance away from the action, Mingo stood with the aid of a wooden cane. "Spur him, Gracia!" he yelled to his granddaughter. "Move him forward. Closer to the steer. Don't let him be lazy!"

Outside the pen, watching through the fence, Matt and Juliet looked at each other and exchanged smiles. After months of rehab, Mingo's speech was almost back to normal. His springy steps were growing steadier every day and only yesterday he'd promised that his cane was going to soon be used as kindling for a spring brushfire.

"Mingo is going to make champions out of both of them," Juliet said with certainty. "Just look at the way Gracia is sitting in that saddle. And Traveler follows her every command."

Matt's green eyes sparkled with love and fatherly pride. "Yes, she's turning into quite a horsewoman. Dad says she and Traveler will be ready to compete in cutting competitions soon."

Juliet's arm slipped across her husband's back as she quietly studied his face. "And how do you feel about that? You're not still fretting? Worrying that something bad will happen to her if she rides?"

A faint smile crossed his face as he gazed thoughtfully out at his father and daughter. "My worries are only those of any normal parent now. This past year I've learned to have faith in my family and faith in God." He glanced at her, his eyes soft with love. "Until you came along, Juliet, I didn't have either. I only saw the darkness around me. I never believed my father could get well. And I never believed I would ever have this much happiness in my life."

Sighing with contentment, she laid her head upon his shoulder and marveled at the change Matt had brought to her life. She would never be alone again. She had a family now, who'd taken her under their wings and made her one of them. She had a daughter who adored her, and a husband who made every day and every night a precious occasion.

"You've made me a pretty happy woman, too, cowboy."

With a knowing grin, his hand reached over and slid a protective hand over her flat stomach. "Don't you think it's time we told everyone about the little one?"

Only yesterday Juliet had gotten the news from her doctor that she was two months pregnant. Matt couldn't have been more thrilled and she knew he was itching to spread their good news.

She pressed a kiss against his cheek and reached for his hand. "Let's start with Mingo and Gracia," she said. "That way the news will spread so quickly that Geraldine will have a barbecue planned for supper tonight."

Laughing, Matt led his wife into the cattle pen and over to his father.

In a matter of seconds, Mingo let out a loud whoop of joy.

* * * * *

Happily ever after is just the beginning...

Turn the page for a sneak preview of
DANCING ON SUNDAY AFTERNOONS
by
Linda Cardillo

Harlequin Everlasting—
Every great love has
a story to tell.™
A brand-new line from Harlequin Books
launching this February!

Prologue

Giulia D'Orazio
1983

I had two husbands—Paolo and Salvatore.

Salvatore and I were married for thirty-two years. I still live in the house he bought for us; I still sleep in our bed. All around me are the signs of our life together. My bedroom window looks out over the garden he planted. In the middle of the city, he coaxed tomatoes, peppers, zucchini—even grapes for his wine—out of the ground. On weekends, he used to drive up to his cousin's farm in Waterbury and bring back manure. In the winter, he wrapped the peach tree and the fig tree with rags and black rubber hoses against the cold, his massive, coarse hands gentling those trees as if they were his fragile-skinned babies. My neighbor, Dominic Grazza, does that for me now. My boys have no time for the garden.

In the front of the house, Salvatore planted roses. The roses I take care of myself. They are giant, cream-colored, fragrant. In the afternoons, I like to sit out on the porch with my coffee, protected from the eyes of the neighborhood by that curtain of flowers.

Salvatore died in this house thirty-five years ago. In the last months, he lay on the sofa in the parlor so he could be in the middle of everything. Except for the two oldest boys, all the children were still at home and we ate together every evening. Salvatore could see the dining room table from the sofa, and he could hear everything that was said. "I'm not dead, yet," he told me. "I want to know what's going on."

When my first grandchild, Cara, was born, we brought her to him, and he held her on his chest, stroking her tiny head. Sometimes they fell asleep together.

Over on the radiator cover in the corner of the parlor is the portrait Salvatore and I had taken on our twenty-fifth anniversary. This brooch I'm wearing today, with the diamonds—I'm wearing it in the photograph also—Salvatore gave it to me that day. Upstairs on my dresser is a jewelry box filled with necklaces and bracelets and earrings. All from Salvatore.

I am surrounded by the things Salvatore gave me, or did for me. But, God forgive me, as I lie alone now in my bed, it is Paolo I remember.

Paolo left me nothing. Nothing, that is, that my family, especially my sisters, thought had any value. No house. No diamonds. Not even a photograph.

But after he was gone, and I could catch my breath from the pain, I knew that I still had something. In the middle of the night, I sat alone and held them in my hands, reading the words over and over until I heard his voice in my head. I had Paolo's letters.

* * * * *

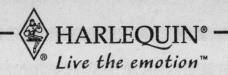

HARLEQUIN®
INTRIGUE®

BREATHTAKING ROMANTIC SUSPENSE

Shared dangers and passions lead to electrifying
romance and heart-stopping suspense!

Every month, you'll meet six new heroes
who are guaranteed to make your spine tingle
and your pulse pound. With them you'll enter
into the exciting world of Harlequin Intrigue—
where your life is on the line
and so is your heart!

THAT'S INTRIGUE—
ROMANTIC SUSPENSE
AT ITS BEST!

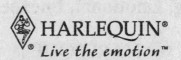

HARLEQUIN®
Live the emotion™

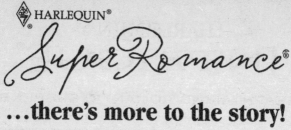
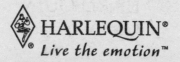

HARLEQUIN®
Presents

The world's bestselling romance series...
The series that brings you your favorite authors,
month after month:

Helen Bianchin...Emma Darcy
Lynne Graham...Penny Jordan
Miranda Lee...Sandra Marton
Anne Mather...Carole Mortimer
Susan Napier...Michelle Reid

and many more uniquely talented authors!

Wealthy, powerful, gorgeous men...
Women who have feelings just like your own...
The stories you love, set in exotic, glamorous locations...

HARLEQUIN®
Presents

Seduction and Passion Guaranteed!

HPDIR104